Tangled In Blue

By

Richard Henshaw

ISBN: 978-0-578-02351-9

*Thanks Angelique, for your patience
and unending support in editing
and publishing this book.
Your ideas helped nurture my
every whim to fruition.*

Thanks Rita, for the excellent research assistance.

To the one woman
who is every woman
in the world to me.

and

For my two biggest fans.
You know who you are.

Tangled in Blue

PART ONE

1

The woman appeared to be deeply engrossed in a book that she was reading. She was curled up on her bed, against a mountain of pillows, wearing only a t-shirt and panties. As she took a sip from her drink, an ice cube spilled from the glass and rolled between her legs. She squirmed to escape the slippery surprise and reached down to find it.

Suddenly, she began to laugh, and she stuck her tongue out at someone who seemed to be in the room with her. She found the melting culprit and was about to pop it into her mouth, when something compelled her to change her mind. Instead, she began to brush the cube across her breasts. Her nipples grew hard from the cold sensation, and it was apparent that she was becoming aroused.

She put the book down and began to rub the ice over the crotch of her panties. She slid her hand inside and quivered, as her fingers glided over her moistening muff. When she removed her hand from it's hidden oasis, the cube was gone. She wriggled out of her panties and slipped her fingers into her opening. She began to undulate on the bed, slowly at first, and then she pressed her hands against herself, as if trying to quell the fever that was beginning to burn within her. She continued to finger herself, and again, she appeared to be conscious of someone that was watching her. She rose to her knees and pushed her hand between her thighs, as she smiled lasciviously for her unseen voyeur.

The woman was definitely enjoying herself, but she was also engaged in the process of acting. She was the lone character in a homemade pornographic movie, and a personal friend of the director of the film. The director's name was Marty, and he was in the process of viewing his work, while engaging in his own form of self gratification. He was masturbating along with the film, and he was very turned on.

Now, on all fours, the woman turned her bum to the camera. It moved in for a close up view, as her fingers glided in and out, and over her glistening mound. There was no sound to the film, but by the look on her face, it was obvious that she was beginning to cum. This was the moment Marty had been waiting for, and it sent him over the edge.

Marty loved to watch women play with themselves, and this particular film was one of several that he'd made for his personal pleasure. The woman in the film was named Selena. She and Marty were once in love. Now, he only had sex with her, so she'd leave him alone. They were both junkies, but booze and heroin had become Selena's lover's, and Marty had become her sugar daddy. Marty had just begun to rewind his film, as Selena walked into the room.

"It's time to take your medicine," she ordered. Marty told her she sounded like a nurse. He sat on the bed and held out his arm. Selena tied his arm with a pair of her panties and pushed the needle into his vein. The drug quickly coursed through him, and he fell back onto his pillow. She had given Marty a much stronger dose than was needed. She was up to something. Selena picked up her panties, and as she stretched them in her hands, she had an idea. She cut up a bed sheet into strips and tied Marty's hands and feet to the bed posts.

Selena glanced at the movie screen and noticed that somehow the film had stopped rewinding, and had paused. What she saw, was a close up of her face, with an expression of orgasmic delight. She snickered and looked at Marty, passed out on the bed. "I wonder what you're thinking about, lover?" Selena walked to her room, grabbed a half empty bottle of vodka and headed for the living room.

2

Perhaps Marty was thinking about his life, and its ups and downs. He may have been thinking about the places he'd been. The love's he'd had, and let slip away. Maybe, he was beginning to feel like his whole life was slipping away and wondering how he'd gotten there.

Marty was born on October 31, 1950 to Frank and Nancy Harrison in Pittsburgh, Pennsylvania. Frank worked in a steel mill, like his father and his grandfather did before him. Nancy was a housewife that saw after Marty and his older brother Stanley and sister LeeAnn. Marty had a fairly normal childhood for a kid whose father was an alcoholic, who regularly beat his wife.

Frank had spent some time in jail as a result of his drinking. As did all the Harrison brothers, at one time or another. Marty's uncles were also heavy drinkers and wife abusers. It was on more than a few occasions that, at least one of the women would have to cover a bruise or a blackened eye with make-up or sunglasses. Holidays, weddings and birthday parties usually turned into a nightmare for Marty and his siblings.

By the time Marty had reached his late teens, he had grown into a rugged, but fairly handsome young guy. He was about six feet tall with an athletic build. He kept his brown hair long or short, however he felt, and with his piercing blue eyes, he had no problem attracting members of the opposite sex.

As Marty got older he played sports, but he began to hang out with a more laid back and hipper crowd. He was into smoking pot and having long rap sessions with people who were more versed in the kind of topics that he was into. He loved to read the works of the beat poets and the writers of the fifties and sixties, whose tales of decadence and freedom of the open road, fueled his dreams to live those same kinds of experiences. In the second half of the sixties, rock music began to take a new direction, with lyrics written in protest and voices that sang about human injustice. Some of the best of that music was coming out of the west coast, particularly in San Francisco. It was his dream to go there someday.

Above all things that Marty felt inside, he was thoroughly attracted to the female gender. He was intrigued and mesmerized by women. As a teenager he had the usual thoughts and feelings fueled by hormones. But Marty's thoughts of women went beyond normalcy, and for most of his life—no matter how good his intentions were—he would struggle and usually fail, to give women the respect that any human being would expect to be entitled to.

Women in the past had always played a submissive role in regards to men and relationships. But that role was changing, and both men and women were a little confused as to what part they played. There were new rules about the way men were to treat women, and the women had to learn to demand it. But deep down inside—and behind closed doors—most women were open to a lot more than they were willing to admit. Most women thought Marty was fun to be with, and they loved him for it. Most of the women in Marty's life had no problem with wearing his boxer shorts.

3

Virginia and Liz were sisters. They were also Harrison's, same as Marty. Marty would come up with all sorts of ways to get in their pants. That they were his cousins, made it even more of a turn on for him.

With long sandy brown hair Virginia was stunningly beautiful. She was older than Marty and Liz, and her demeanor was cold and sullen. She used Marty for her own satisfaction, and you could say that she showed him the ropes. She was his first sexual partner, and she taught him how to please a woman. She explained the female anatomy to him and what turned a woman on.

Marty learned well. When Virginia turned her attentions to his friend Alex, she asked him to set them up. He told her that he would, but only if she continued to fuck him, too. She agreed, and even though she and Alex dated for several months, he never knew about their little arrangement.

Virginia's sister was a different story altogether. Liz had the hots for Marty. She always told him that she wished they could see each other openly. Marty liked her, too. She had blond hair and kittenish green eyes. Outwardly, she seemed like a good girl, and she was. But under the sheets she was real bad, fucking like an animal in heat.

Liz was his best friend, and they were always together. She even liked sports. She was a cheerleader, but she had played pick-up ball with the guys since she was a kid. She quit playing football when she began to fill out, and the guys started trying to cop a feel.

When their relationship began to turn sexual, it felt completely natural, as though no line had been crossed at all. By the time she turned seventeen, Liz had become Marty's idea of perfection in a woman, both physically and emotionally. But she was his cousin, and he didn't take her seriously as a love interest, like she did him. As close as they were, he would inevitably hurt her many times.

One day they were swimming at her house. Liz had gone in to take a shower. She had just sat down on the toilet when Marty came into the room. He slid out of his swim trunks, and he was already hard. Liz was peeing, as he walked toward her, and she began to suck his cock.

Marty told her to stand up, and he knelt in front of her. He caught a drop of pee with his tongue and buried his face into her glistening muff. Soon they were laying on the floor, and she lowered herself onto him. As Liz began to cum, she told Marty that she loved him. He pushed her off of him and said sarcastically, "I love you, too, Cuz," and he got up and left.

4

In high school, Marty went steady with a hippie girl named Kirstin. She liked to get naked and run through the woods. They loved to camp out and smoke pot and make love by the fire. Marty played on the baseball and football teams and Kirstin cheered him on. She'd wait by the locker room door for him to come out, and then they'd go out with the gang for pizza or burgers. He gave her a promise ring, and they talked about getting married after they graduated.

The young lovers had gone on a hayride with some friends, and as the gang sat by the fire roasting marshmallows, the two of them slipped away. Kirstin laid in the wagon, watching Marty, as his tongue darted in and out of her vagina. She ran her fingers through his hair and wondered if the others would miss them. But soon, the licking he had been giving her started to make her forget all about that, and she pulled him to her.

As they made love, their favorite song began to waft from a transistor radio that someone had brought along for the ride. Marty's rhythmic thrusts seemed to be moving in time to the music, and it wasn't long before she could feel herself beginning to cum. She held onto his buttocks and tried to meet him halfway with each intensifying wave of pleasure, clenching him tight, as her climax rushed through her sated loins.

As Marty rolled off of her and pulled up his pants, Kirstin laid breathless under the stars above. She could feel the cool evening breeze between her legs, and she quietly hoped it could be this way forever. She pulled her pants back on, and they joined their friends by the fire.

A few months later, Kirstin's father's company transferred him to Chicago, and she moved away. She called Marty a few times after that, but each conversation became shorter than the last, until she finally stopped calling. Marty never tried to call her.

Marty graduated high school, and when he turned eighteen he got a job in the steel mill. He began to hit the bottle hard, and he started getting into bar fights and scrapes with the law. He seemed to be following in the family tradition to the letter.

His uncles had always gotten alcohol for him. But as Marty and his friends got older, they had no problem finding a watering hole to down a few cold beers. There were plenty of fine drinking establishments, where customers could find a bartender, who would turn a blind eye to their age and serve them their favorite beverage.

It was around this time that his family fell into a period of very sad circumstances. Marty's uncle Kevin suddenly committed suicide. No one could understand why, because he seemed to be happy and he always smiled. Then, Virginia and Liz's dad was diagnosed with cirrhosis of the liver, and he wasn't given long to live. Uncle Wilbur could be an especially mean man, if he felt like it. Once, when Marty was about twelve years old, his uncle sat in his chair and laughed, as his pet doberman growled and snarled at his feet. Scared shitless, Marty sat on the couch and tried not to show his fear, until his uncle finally called the dog off of him.

Four months later, Marty's parents were killed in an automobile accident. The operator of a tractor trailer lost control of his rig, and it rolled over several cars on the highway. Theirs was the last one it hit. Marty's brother Stanley was away at college, and his sister LeeAnn lived down in Florida with her husband Wayne. It was up to Marty to make the calls.

Even though Marty never cared much for his father, he felt bad just the same. He'd loved his mother and would grieve for her for the rest of his life. It was hard for him to make all of the arrangements. Once LeeAnn and Stan got home, it was easier. Frank and Nancy had wished to be cremated and the minister performed a double ceremony.

Liz stayed by Marty's side at the funeral. They talked about having three deaths in four months. "This town is dead for me!" he cried. Liz told him that she was moving to the west coast to attend classes at Berkeley. "I'm leaving next week," she said.

"Great for you," Marty replied. "I'm gonna be outta here, too!"

"Oh, yeah...where ya goin'?"

"I'll find out when I get there."

Two weeks later, Marty quit his job at the mill and went down to enlist in the Army. His friends told him that he was crazy, that he was committing suicide. "Maybe I am," Marty told his friend Paul, as they sat at the bar. He took a long drink of his beer and said, "Maybe I wanna die! Besides...I'll probably get drafted anyway!"

"But there is needless, wanton killing goin' on man! The war is wrong, and we're gonna put a stop to it! I thought you were cool, man! I thought you were one of us!"

"I ain't part of nothing, man! I'm on my own... and maybe I want to kill somebody!" Paul looked at him in disbelief, and then Marty said, "Give me a cigarette, man."

"Fuck you, Marty! You're one of them! I hope I don't see you around!" Paul left Marty sitting there.

But Marty wasn't stupid. He'd signed up to be a supply clerk, hoping that he wouldn't be involved in any front line combat. And he really did believe the war was wrong. He wasn't cut out to be a soldier. He just wanted to get away. He was at a crossroad in his life, where he was confused and feeling sorry for himself. Everyone was either dying or leaving town. One way or another, Marty would do the same.

5

Marty had a couple of weeks, before he was due to leave for boot camp. He'd heard about a big three day concert up in Bethel, New York. Two years before, there had been one like it in California. This one was said to be bigger yet. He called his friend Nelson Piroli, and they bought four tickets. Nelson's steady girlfriend Beth Ferguson would go, and Marty invited his cousin Virginia. Beth was a feisty red head with a gorgeous body and a naughty sense of humor. Marty had the hots for Beth, and Virginia could tell. "Stay down, boy!" she teased.

Nelson had been Marty's friend since they were kids. They were opposites in some ways. Marty only studied what he liked in school, while Nelson studied everything. Marty loved to have long conversations with Nelson because he would explain things in a way that he could understand. In high school, Nelson played on the basketball team, and was very popular. At parties, people would gather around him because he'd always have something interesting to say.

Nelson had a '67 Chevy Nova. The four of them jumped in, and up to New York they drove. The ride up was free sailing, until they got close to the sight. There, they found themselves in a huge traffic jam. Nothing was moving and people were partying right there in the road. Some people began to leave their cars and walk the rest of the way. Marty and Nelson decided to do the same. "What about your car?" asked Virginia.

"Fuck it!" Marty said giddily.

"We'll get it later," Nelson told her ."You think someone is gonna take it outta here?" They started walking, and the girls followed.

What they saw when they got there was an amazing sight to behold. A sea of people was nestled in a giant valley, and the music was already wafting through the air. No one took their tickets—it had become a free show. The scene was incredible. It was everything that the promoters had boasted. Not long after they'd settled in, someone gave them some 'LSD'. It was the drug everyone had been using to expand their mind and see the light.

Three days of peace, love and music, and sliding in the mud. People getting naked and making love with whoever was sitting next to them. Marty wandered off with a girl named Blossom. They had sex under a grove of apple trees. It reminded Marty of Adam and Eve, when Blossom picked an apple and offered him a bite.

The music was unbelievable. Marty stayed stoned the whole time. At one point, he'd passed out and when he awoke, Blossom had left him. He looked for Nelson and the girls, but there were so many people, it would have been a miracle if he had found them. He'd lost his friends, and at the end, he hitchhiked home, alone.

6

The time had come for Marty to go and serve his country. To
protect its people, so they could be free to do great things like the
festival he'd just experienced. Actually, Marty had been thinking more
about the government benefits he'd receive after he got out. Like G.I.
loans and preference on jobs like the postal service. Marty could see
himself as a mailman, delivering packages to pretty housewives. Of
course this all depended on whether he came back in one piece.

He boarded a greyhound bus headed to Fort Leonard Wood,
Missouri. On the way, he looked at this fellow passengers and
wondered where they were going. An older man, a hippie and a guy
who looked like he just of out of prison. Marty wasn't sure why he
thought that about the guy, except that he had that look. Like someone
who had just been set free and had forgotten what to do with that
freedom.

Marty knew that by joining the Army, his freedom was about to be taken away. Had he made a mistake? He looked out the window of the bus. Out towards the open fields and the hills beyond. He turned his attention to a pretty young girl sitting a few seats in front of him. He wondered where she was going, and he wished that he was going with her.

The bus left Pittsburgh at night and continued on through the next day, changing buses twice. At the bus stations, Marty smoked cigarettes and drank coffee, and again he wondered what other people's stories were. He saw bums sleeping on benches, and cops who chased them away. One guy asked Marty for some change, and he gave him five bucks and a pack of cigarettes. He thought that even though a vagabond was free of the material restraints of the rat race, he didn't have the means to enjoy it. Did they purposely live this kind of life, or were they castaways from the dream of the white picket fence.

It was nightfall when the bus pulled up to the Fort Leonard Wood reception station. To Marty's surprise, two other guys and a girl got off with him. He'd assumed that he was the only one on the bus who was giving the next couple of years of his life to Uncle Sam. He realized that they were all a little nervous about what they were getting themselves into. Not one of them would look at the others, as the sergeant led them into the first building.

They spent the next two days at the reception center with recruits who had come from all over the country. Marty was surprised at how laid back it seemed compared to the horror stories he'd heard.

They filled out forms and went to the barber. Marty watched some long hair get cut off of a few girls' heads, and a few guys, too. They were issued uniforms and equipment, and were given a small advance on their pay to buy personal items, like soap and toothpaste. Marty bought a wristwatch and some books to read. They played pool and drank beer, and even went to a movie.

The day the bus came to take them to their company barracks was different. The ride over was calm and uneventful. The drill sergeants smoked their cigarettes and barely looked at them. But when the bus stopped at the barracks, and the doors opened, all hell broke loose. One drill sergeant flicked his cigarette to the floor. Another flicked his at a recruit. They all started yelling to get off the bus. They grabbed and threw people out of the bus, and onto the ground. They literally kicked guys in the ass and ordered them to run up to the sergeants, who were standing in front of the building. They in turn would send everyone back down. This went on and on, and almost resulted in total mayhem. They especially picked on a heavy set guy, and at one point, he stumbled and fell, and his duffle bag burst open. A bunch of snacks and lunch-cakes fell out on the sidewalk, and a drill sergeant shouted with glee, "Oh, now look what I found!" The guy became their personal lap dog for sometime to come.

They ordered everyone into a formation and made them do hundreds of pushups. By the time they had made it into the barracks, and things began to settle down, Marty saw grown men sitting there crying like babies. He was a long way from the festival where, at the end, he and a few hundred stragglers had built a huge peace sign from the debris that was left behind. Now, as he watched the crying men, he could only mutter to himself, "What the hell have I gotten myself into?"

After a few weeks, Marty started to adapt and thought it wasn't that bad at all. To fight for freedom, he'd basically given up all of his constitutional rights. He was now government property. But the Army practically ran his life for him, and all he had to do was go with the flow. Still, during his whole time in the military, he would never feel like a soldier, and he just basically enjoyed the ride.

7

After a month, the recruits were given a weekend pass. Marty
tried to go without shaving, and almost had his pass revoked. He and a
few of his buddies went into town, and straight to a club. They were
buying drinks left and right for girls at the bar, when Marty realized
that they were employees, and coaxed one to admit it.

Next stop was a tattoo parlor. Marty had a skull with roses
around it, done on his back. It was the first of many tattoos that would
eventually adorn his body. The town was full of clubs and bars, so
Marty and the guys started hopping from one to another.

Soon, Marty found himself sitting at the bar of a dance hall,
with a rock band playing. He was starting to get drunk. He noticed a
woman standing next to him, and he started a conversation with her.
Her name was Katie Rawlins. She told Marty that she lived close to
town, and that she loved to party on the weekends. Marty could tell

that she was a few years older than him. But she was gorgeous. They got drunk together and danced all night. At one point, Marty tried to kiss her, and he fell off his barstool. Katie helped him up, the two of them laughing hysterically.

They left the bar, and Katie drove them to her place. She told Marty that she was divorced, and when they arrived at her house, she introduced him to her mother and her two teenage daughters. They all talked for a while, and soon her mother and the girls went to bed.

Katie laid a couple of blankets and pillows down on the floor. Marty lifted her sweater off of her and fumbled with her bra. She helped him out and finished undressing herself. Marty was right behind her. They began to kiss, and he brushed his hand down her belly to her now soaked muff. Katie begged him to put his cock inside of her. He did, and began to push in and out of her, hard and fast. She pushed him off and climbed on top of him. Within minutes she began to cum. Marty sensed that she was getting off, and he let himself go.

They snuggled together and talked for a while, then Katie began to suck Marty back to attention. She climbed on top, and he pushed himself into her. She smiled, as she slid up and down his swollen shaft. Marty pressed into her, and she slammed down against him. As their lovemaking intensified, Katie's smile disappeared, and she began to moan. She gasped with each stroke, and soon she could feel her orgasm coming. As the waves of her climax began to wane, she fell on top of him.

Katie laid there on his chest for awhile, panting. She pushed herself up, and her smile returned. Out of the corner of his eye, Marty noticed something move. It was Katie's mother watching them from the hallway. She saw him notice her, and she disappeared. Marty didn't bother to tell Katie, even though he wondered what the old woman was up to. The sated lovers talked a while more. She said that she liked his tattoo, and that she hoped that he would spend the rest of the weekend with her. He told her that he would, and after awhile Katie fell asleep.

Marty laid awake, because he suddenly had a weird feeling that something wasn't right. All kinds of scenarios began rolling around in his head and he started to think that Katie wasn't really divorced. He started to think that maybe her husband was just out of town. A lot of military wive's whored around on their husbands. "What if her husband was in Vietnam, and she was out getting laid every weekend, until he came home?"

Marty would never know for sure. He laid there awhile longer, until he was sure that she was asleep, and then he quietly gathered his clothes and slipped out the door.

8

Marty made it through boot camp and learned a few things along the way. He even started to learn how to play the guitar, thanks to his friend Earl, who was from Tennessee. Earl showed Marty some chords and a few picking techniques, and let him use his guitar to practice. Marty had bought a harmonica, and Earl helped him out with that too. Marty would make a lot of friends like Earl during the next couple of years. And then he would never see them again.

The heavy-set guy, who lost his chips and cupcakes in the beginning, made it too. At first, Seth couldn't do three push-ups. "I'm weak sergeant...I can't do anymore!" he'd whine.

"That's why I'm here son!" the drill sergeant would reply. "To condition your mind and body!"

And condition his mind and body they did. Seth had turned his fat into muscle, and as it turned out, he was intelligent as well. Seth was another good friend that Marty had made, and they had helped each other make it through.

Everyone got their orders, and most were headed to Vietnam, including Marty. He figured it was the end of the good times. But then out of a sudden turn of events, his orders were changed. He was going to Germany instead. Marty jumped for joy. "Frauleins, instead of Rice Paddies!" he laughed.

Because of the change of orders, he had to stay in Missouri another week. During that time Marty found out that the drill sergeants were really human after all. All that yelling and cursing and spitting was just an act. It was their job to turn wimps into lean mean killing machines. Their main objective was to win the war, but it was also to try and keep the young men from coming home in a body bag. They turned out to be just regular guys, and they even let Marty watch from an upstairs window, as the new meat came in.

Marty had two weeks leave time, so he took a bus to Jacksonville, Florida to visit his sister LeeAnn and husband Wayne. Their daughter Summer was almost two years old now. Wayne was an anesthesiologist at a hospital and LeeAnn was a real estate agent. It was a time when women were beginning to have a career, and still be a mother and housewife as well.

LeeAnn was seven years older than Marty. The two of them had never been real close. "My how big my little niece is getting!" Marty cooed, as he held Summer in his arms. They talked the usual small talk, and LeeAnn said, "Marty, I thought you were nuts when you joined up. I figured you were gonna come home dead. Thank heaven that they changed your orders."

She meant it, and Marty was glad to know that she cared about him. He stayed at LeeAnn and Wayne's for a couple of days, eating good and loafing around. In the evenings they listened to music and drank beer. Wayne played guitar, and Marty got out his harmonica and jammed with him.

The next stop for Marty was back home in Pittsburgh. He didn't know why he called it home—he really didn't have one there anymore. He took a plane this time, and made it there in a couple of hours. He stayed at his grandparents house and hung out with Nelson in the bars at night.

Nelson was forever going to college and talking about growing pot. "Hydroponics man... that's where it's at!" he would say. Marty just laughed, but he knew Nelson was very intelligent. He had a very high IQ and a photographic memory. He told Marty, "Our minds work like a computer...constantly gathering and storing data. We just haven't figured out how to tap into the full extent of the process." Some of the things that Nelson said astounded Marty. But he also knew when Nelson was full of shit. On occasion, when he would talk about outer space, Marty could almost swear that he heard it all before. In a science fiction movie.

9

    It was October, and autumn in the northeast was a beautiful and scenic time. The leaves on the trees went through amazing changes in color, and pumpkin patches were plentiful. Halloween was coming, and in the spirit of the season, Marty and Nelson decided to drive up north to Salem, Massachusetts. Nelson had managed to retrieve his car after the festival, just as it was about to be towed. They filled it with gas, and they picked up Nelson's girlfriend Beth, and then they were on their way.

    The further they headed north, the more beautiful the scenery became. Marty loved the fall, but he hated that winter followed it. By nature he was never the cheerful type, and every year, as wintertime came he would get the blues. It was a dark and dreary time for him. Most people he knew from western Pennsylvania loved the seasons, winter included. Not Marty. He always said that he would eventually move to the southwest and stay there for good.

On this trip the weather was just magnificent. They decided to go to Niagara Falls and spend the night. They had a good meal and hit a few bars, then they got a welcome nights sleep, after their long day. In the morning, they went for breakfast, and then they went to see the Falls. With the colorful backdrop the view was spectacular. They drove all of that day and made it to Salem by late evening.

They had dinner and walked around for a while. There had typically, through the years, been stories of ghost's that haunted the region. Restless spirits, who had wandered the countryside as a result of a sudden or violent death. As the three ghost-hunters ventured into a secluded part of town, they came upon a cemetery. Shadows moved in the cool night air, and slowly they began to get the creeps. "I've got just the cure for all of your fears," Nelson assured his friends. He procured a joint from the pocket of his jacket, and the three began to get high. As the drug took effect, they started to loosen up, and they laughed out loud.

Suddenly, Nelson cringed in mock fright. "What was that?" he cried.

"It's right behind us!" Marty chimed.

Beth screamed, "All right you guys! That'll be enough! You're scaring the crap outta me!"

They all laughed, and then Marty yelled, "There goes one now!" Instantly, they took off running up the street, screaming and laughing. As they came upon an entrance to a tavern, Marty said,

"Quick...in here!"

The place was called 'The Settlers Inn', and was known to harbor a few spirits of it's own. They found a table, and Nelson went up to the bar to order some beer. As Beth and Marty took their seats, Marty's dirty mind began to take over. The excitement and cool air had caused Beth's nipples to harden. "I see you've got your high-beams on," he teased.

"What did you say? What's that supposed to mean?"

"Well...it's just that...well..."

Beth could see that Marty was looking at her chest. "Oh, I see. My high-beams. Oh, yeah. Well... is it time for the baby's nursing?"

Marty's eyes lit up. He'd wanted Beth since high school, and she had flirted with him plenty of times. She chided him, "You're a child Marty. Grow up!"

Nelson returned with the beer, and they got down to some serious drinking. The place began to fill up, and soon it was so crowded they could barely move. A group of people filled the table next to theirs, and it became a party. Everyone was getting loaded, and when Beth made her way to the bar, Marty followed. He sidled up next to her and put his arm around her waist.

"Don't!" she said, and she shooed him aside with her hip. Suddenly, the crowd pushed in around them. He moved behind her and pressed himself against her bum. "Marty! Leave me..." Before Beth could finish, he had opened her jeans and slid his hand into her panties. She didn't try to stop him. She was really drunk, and her

29

defenses were down. She sighed, as he pushed his fingers inside of her. They were tight against the bar, and no one could see what they were doing. No one even had time to notice. They were all engrossed in their own form of revelry. Marty continued, and soon Beth turned her head and whispered into his ear that she was about to cum. He watched in the mirror behind the bar, as the look on her face became wrought with pleasure. She reached down and pressed her hand over his, and helped him finish the job.

Marty and Beth needn't have worried about poor Nelson all alone at the table. Busy partying with their new found friends, he had slipped outside to get high. But Nelson had stayed out there a lot longer than the others. While Marty and Beth were having their fun, Nelson was out in the parking lot, screwing someone in the back of her station wagon.

Somehow the three of them managed to stagger back to their motel room. Nelson hit the bed and went out like a light. Beth was so trashed that the last thing Marty remembered, was seeing her crawling across the floor on her hands and knees, and puking her guts out.

The next day they set out to see the sights, all the while nursing some tremendous hangovers. As the day went by they began to feel better and they went to the museum and took in a tour. The host of the tour explained in detail the different ways that young girls—and even old men—were tortured into confessing that they were witches. Beth thought it was more sad than scary. They took a break to eat dinner. Marty and Nelson ordered seafood, and Beth almost became sick from the smell of it. Her stomach still hadn't settled from the night before, and she hardly touched her meal.

After dinner they attended 'A Ghostly Gathering.' Everyone sat around a cozy bonfire and listened, as the host spun tales of witches and goblins. They had cookies and apple cider, and a few people roasted hot dogs over the fire. Jack-o-lanterns were lit all around. Marty liked ghost stories and horror movies. He had a definite interest in the dark side and had even fantasized about being a vampire, seducing beautiful young women, before draining them of just enough blood to turn them into vampires as well.

10

Marty had a lot of fantasies, and when he accidentally walked in on Beth while she was taking a shower, fantasy became reality. The three of them had come back from the bonfire, and Marty had dozed off in the chair. In the meantime, Nelson had decided to go out for cigarettes and beer. When Marty woke up, the place was quiet, and it seemed as if he was all alone. He got up and headed to the bathroom to take a pee. Beth had partially opened the door to let the steam out from the shower. Marty pushed the door open, and when he saw her drying off, he lost control.

At first, Beth covered herself. "Marty!" she squealed, "what do you think you're doing! Nelson will be coming back any minute!"

Marty was determined. "We have time," he assured her. As he came toward her, he began to undo his pants and push them down. Beth could see he was already hard. He grabbed her towel and threw it on the floor. She backed into the wall, and that was right where he wanted her. He began to kiss her, and she bit hard into his lip. Marty didn't stop, and he tried to push his hardened penis into her. "Oh, shit, Marty...Don't..." she whimpered. But it was a half-hearted last attempt to stop him. She already knew that she was going to let him do it.

Their wild breathing echoed in the small bathroom, as Beth grabbed Marty's cock and guided him into her vagina. He pushed hard, up into her, and she gasped in pain and ecstasy. Marty slammed in and out of her, almost lifting her into the air. Beth's knees began to buckle, but he held her up and she wrapped her legs around him.

In minutes, Marty began to feel the familiar rumbling within his loins, and he quickly pulled himself out of her. He carried her to the sink and let her down. Beth knew what he wanted. She turned and held on to the sink, arching her behind into the air, offering herself to him. He got behind her and pushed himself in. This time he teased her, pulling the length of his shaft in and out, letting it rub against her clitoris.

In a split second, she thought about Nelson coming back. She knew that she should stop what she was doing. She was glad that the mirror above the sink was fogged, and she couldn't see her face. "Please, Marty!" she begged. "Hurry up and cum!"

He started to push himself faster and told her how good it felt to have his cock inside of her. Despite her feelings of guilt, it felt good to Beth, too, and she reached down and rubbed her clit. Marty began to fill her up inside. "Whew, it's about time!" she said, relieved that it was over. She was still breathing hard when she heard the door open.

Marty quickly pulled out of her and tried to get his pants up. Beth went scrambling for her towel, but by the that time, Nelson was standing in the bathroom doorway. Without saying a word, he punched Marty in the mouth, and hit him three more times as he went down. Nelson was a peace loving guy, but this was more than he could stand. Beth just stood there in shock, holding her towel up to her mouth and biting it. Nelson looked at her for a few seconds, and then he slapped her in the face. She cowered into the corner and started to cry. Nelson shook his head and left the room.

Beth slid down the wall and sat on the floor. She looked at Marty laying there unconscious, and suddenly an extreme anger welled up inside of her. She crawled over to Marty and began to slap and punch his head. "You Bastard!" she cried. "You sick, fucking bastard! I hate you, fucker! I hate you!"

But even though Marty had started it, she let him do it, and she liked it. It was the time of year when the leaves fell, and the flowers wilted and died. Beth knew that a good thing had just died, and it was her own fault. She began to hit herself in the head and pull her hair. Marty's dark world was beginning to spread it's foul wings. And the people he loved the most would have their very lives sucked out of them along the way. Maybe he really was a vampire, after all.

Beth got dressed, and set out to look for Nelson, half afraid of what he might do when she found him. She was relieved to see that his car was outside, and that he was on foot. Considering the events of

34

the evening, she had a pretty fair idea where he might have gone, and in spite of the lateness of the hour, she got up the courage to take a walk and see where her intuitive powers would lead her.

As she made her way to the inn, the stories of spirits and witchcraft began to play on her mind. Leaves skipped past her in the breeze, and tree limbs seemed to cast eerie shadows across the moonlit streets. The lights of the inn were a welcome sight, and she began to pick up her pace, until she had made it up the steps and safely inside.

The place was empty compared to the night before, and Beth quickly realized that Nelson wasn't there. She found a seat at the bar and ordered a beer. "Maybe he'll show up," she sighed. Seven beers and six tequila's later, she decided that he wasn't coming. As she stepped down from her chair, she stumbled, and when the guy sitting next to her tried to help, she shoved him away. "I ain't worried about a couple of ghosts," she slurred. "My boyfriend will kick their ass!"

When she got back to the motel, Marty told her that Nelson had never returned. She excused herself to the bathroom, and as she sat there, everything began to spin. Beth never could hold her alcohol, and as if on schedule, she emptied the contents of her stomach into the toilet.

For the next hour or so, they sat awake, smoking cigarettes and drinking the beer that Nelson had bought. They barely spoke a word to each other. Marty tried to say that he was sorry, but all Beth had to say was, "Fuck You." They both finally fell asleep, her on the bed, and him in the chair.

In the morning they looked outside and Nelson was leaning on the car, waiting. He had walked around for most of the night wondering why his woman and his best friend would do this to him. And at the moment, he hated them for it. But in the back of his mind, he remembered doing Beth just as wrong. Only a couple of nights before, his dick had been between the legs of another woman, and it wasn't the first time. Still, he felt he'd been made a fool, and he couldn't forgive them for that. "If you ain't in this car in ten seconds, I'm gone!" he commanded.

The guilty duo grabbed their stuff, and when they tried to get into the car, Nelson backed up and almost knocked Beth on the ground. "Get in!" he yelled again, and this time he let them get in the car. It was a long, silent ride home. Nelson only stopped once, when Beth was about to wet herself. Marty got hard right there in the back seat, as he pictured what it would be like to see Beth pee her pants.

PART TWO

1

The plane began its taxi down the runway, Marty was both nervous and excited about what lay ahead of him. What he was leaving behind at the moment were some things he'd just as soon forget. But he knew that he wouldn't. He still had a black eye and a sore jaw from getting his clock cleaned by Nelson. Marty knew that he'd hurt a good friend and figured Nelson would never forgive him. It was an eight hour flight to Frankfurt. Marty slept most of the way. He spent the rest of the time reading and talking with a beautiful German girl that was sitting next to him. Her name was Claudia, and she spoke perfect English.

She told Marty that she was from a small town in Frankfurt, and that she had just spent the past year in New York. She had been staying with relatives and had taken some college classes. She'd had a job in a hair salon and said that she took pride in following the etiquette of the American woman. "You see," she said, "in Europe most women don't bother to shave their legs or under their arms."

"Oh, really. Well, that kind of stuff is no big deal to me."

Marty had heard that before. In America, women were held to a higher standard of vanity. Men expected them to be every bit of sugar and spice and everything nice. Marty liked his women to smell good, but he had no hang-ups about underarm foliage. He was a little unsure about hairy legs though.

Marty was interested in what Claudia had to say. He figured that it would give him a heads up on things once he got there. He was even more interested in how she looked. She could have been a centerfold model in a men's magazine. By now, all Marty really wanted was to have sex with her right there on the plane. He told her that he was in the Army, and that he was on his way to Frankfurt, himself. "Maybe we could hook up sometime," he said.

"Hook up? What does this mean...hook up?"

Marty laughed, "It's the same as hang out, or get together. You know...like a date."

"Ohh!" she said with a laugh. "Maybe, you never know..."

They enjoyed each other's company the rest of the flight, and Claudia tried to teach Marty some of the German language. "Ein beer, bitte" was the first thing he needed to know. He'd heard about the very strong beer they had in Europe, and he couldn't wait to try it. Claudia made Marty forget about things for a while, and Germany was looking pretty good from where he sat at the moment.

2

When they landed in Frankfurt, Marty had to say goodbye to
Claudia. He had to go to the Rhein Mein Air Force base that was right
next to the airport. He was surprised at how laid back it seemed now
that he was dealing with regular Army personnel. He still had to mind
his 'esprit de corps' and remember to salute officers. But it was like
night and day compared to boot camp. Marty and a few others
attended an orientation session and spent the night on the base. There
was an 'Enlisted Club' nearby, so Marty and a guy named Pat relaxed
and tried out the beer.

The both of them were going to be stationed at Camp
Eschborn. It was a small post occupied by just one battalion of combat
engineers. Pat was a heavy equipment operator. He ran bulldozers
and front end loaders. Marty and Pat were both assigned to
Headquarters Company.

Pat Wilson was his full name, and he was from Colorado Springs, Colorado. Marty noticed that the tip of Pat's middle finger was missing. He would later tell him that he'd stuck his finger into a running fan as a kid, because his brother had dared him to. He would also eventually tell Marty that he hated his mother, and that they didn't speak to each other. He never told him why.

The next day, when they arrived at Camp Eschborn they were assigned to a Sergeant Fleishmann. He would help to process them in and pick up their equipment. Sergeant Fleishmann, or Bill was in the process of processing out. He had finished his tour of duty, and was headed home in a couple of weeks. "I'm headed back to the world," he told them.

Pat said, "Back to the world?"

"Yeah...you know. It's been fun around here, but after a while you get bored," he explained. "It's kinda like being stuck on an island. I mean...these people over here...they kinda do their own thing. In the good old U.S.A. you can have it all. Dig what I'm sayin' man?"

Bill informed Marty and Pat that practically everyone on the post was a heroin junkie. He said he could get them some. Marty was interested, but Pat said he'd pass. "I like my beer... and I'll smoke a little grass."

"No problem," Bill replied, "I can get you some hashish."
Pat was up for that. He was a little bit suspicious of Bill, though. He told Marty that he seemed a little shaky.

"Aw, he's cool," Marty assured him.

40

"Ya think so, huh?"

That night Bill took Marty and Pat into the city of Frankfurt and showed them around. It was an unbelievable night to say the least. They converted their money into Deutschemarks and hit the bars for some serious beer drinking. After a couple of hours, they went to meet their connection. Bill led them to an old apartment building, and they went upstairs.

He knocked on the door, and a woman asked them to come inside. She was a prostitute Bill had gotten to know, and she had the good stuff. Bill did most of the talking, because he could speak fluent German. The woman shook her head, and he told Pat that she didn't have any hashish. He was disappointed. Bill told Marty to fork over fifty marks, and he gave the money to the woman. She fixed Bill up, first. Marty and Pat watched, as she tied his arm and tapped it with her fingers. She pushed the needle in and loosened the tie. When she was finished, Bill walked over to a chair and sat down. He stared straight ahead, like he was in a trance. Marty was next. The woman prepared his fix and called him over. As the drug coursed through his veins, he experienced a feeling of warmth throughout his body. He staggered backwards and sat down on her bed. He was overcome with a feeling of well being like never before. All of his cares had dissolved in a single moment. Marty thought that he wouldn't mind staying like this forever.

As the initial sensation began to subside, he tried to focus and clear his perception. He stood up, with Pat's assistance, but everything seemed to be in slow motion. "You okay?" Pat asked.

"I feel great. This is out of this world." Marty looked for Bill and saw that he was gone.

"He left..took off downstairs," Pat told him.

"We must find him, then."

They said goodbye to the woman, and then Marty thanked her. "Danke," he said.

"Yeah, yeah," she replied in her German accent, shooing them out the door.

When they stepped outside, they saw Bill staggering around and pointing a pistol at everyone that walked by. "Where the hell did he get that?" Pat asked in total amazement. Bill started mumbling about getting someone, and then he fell against a garbage can. Marty and Pat picked him up and told him to put the gun away. He spun around and pointed it into the street. Marty thought that the gun was going to go off at any second. He ran over to Bill and wrestled it out of his hand. It was the first time he got a good look at the weapon. It was an Army Issue .45. It was loaded, but the safety was on. "The cops are gonna be here any minute!" said Pat. "Let's get the hell outta here!"

Suddenly, Bill seemed to snap out of it and said, "I'm alright. Gimme my gun."

Pat protested, "He's crazy, Marty!"

Marty reluctantly gave the gun to Bill. He put it in his back pack, and they walked to a pub down the street. After a couple of beers, Bill pulled the gun out and laid it on the bar. Pat said, "I've had enough of this shit!" and walked out.

Marty yelled, "Pat...wait!" He asked Bill if he'd be alright, if they left.

"Go on," Bill told him. "I know the people in here. I got a score to settle."

Marty had no idea what he was talking about, but he said, "I'll see ya Bill," and went after Pat. He found him at the corner, hailing a taxi cab. He jumped in behind him and told the driver, "Take us to Sachsenhausen."

Sachsenhausen was a section of the city that was most popular for the young crowd to party. The intrepid pair hit a few pubs and listened to some really good bands. Pat felt a lot better now that they were rid of Bill. But Marty was getting more and more loaded himself, and at one point, he fell off his barstool. A German man and woman helped him up and bought him a beer.

Everyone was laughing, and Marty suddenly became unsure if they were laughing with him, or at him. Even worse, when he looked around Pat was gone. He went outside and sat on some steps and watched several guys brawling in an alley. He began to vomit and realized he'd had enough.

Marty caught a taxi cab, and tried to tell the driver where to go. The next thing he knew, he was waking up in a field and had no idea where he was. He noticed the 'Polizei' sitting in a patrol car nearby. Marty tried to speak to them in German, using his little guide book that he had carried with him. As he stumbled over the words, the cops just laughed. "See that tower over there," one said in English. "That's where you want to go." Marty was stunned that the cop knew how to speak English. But he was glad that he did. "Danke," he said, thanking them and staggered his way back to his bed.

Marty would find out that most Germans under the age of thirty could speak English. It was a required course for them in school. But like in any country, the people expected visitors to try and speak their language first. Marty learned as much as he could. It was a good way to meet girls, by asking them to teach him how to say things like, "How are you? May I sit here with you? Would you like another drink?" and cultural questions like that.

He made a few friends and had many discussions with young people his age, who were really not happy about the U.S Military being in their country. He saw their point of view, but he also tried to remind them of how the Americans had come to be there in the first place. "That's all well and good," one guy told Marty, "but we don't want your nuclear missiles here!"

He even told them that he wasn't into being a soldier. "I just joined the Army to travel and see places like this," he explained. Some of them found him to be a hypocrite for having an attitude like that. Marty settled into his military life and found that it was almost like a regular job. At work he issued all types of things from weapons and ammo, to blankets and pillows.

He had to pull guard duty every now and then, and a few times a year they went into the 'field' and practiced first aid and target shooting. They simulated combat scenarios and built bridges and airstrips. Marty made friends with some really good guys while he was there. One such friendship was cemented through an unlikely succession of events that changed his life for the better. Marty was sitting in the headquarters tool shed in the motor pool. He was kicked back, smoking a cigarette, when a Buck Sergeant walked up and stood in the doorway. "Get da he-ll off-a yo duff!" he ordered, stomping his foot. Marty had never seen the man before. He was a big black guy with a deep southern drawl.

"Who says it?" he asked lazily.

"Sergeant Andre Ward...Dat's who!"

"I'm on break. And, besides...who died and left you boss?"

Sergeant Ward's face lit up like a half stick of dynamite. "Tell me I didn't just hear you say dat, Corporal! If you don't get off-a dat chair right now...I'm gonna write yo' dead ass up!"

Marty had been sticking a putty knife into the work bench, and just as Andre finished his tirade, he threw it, aiming for the door frame next to his head. It stuck into the wood right past his ear. Andre jumped back and looked at Marty in amazement. "What da fuck!" he exclaimed, his voice rising a few octaves. "Da first sergeant's gonna hear about dis!" Marty could hear him mumbling, as he walked away. "Dat one, crazy mutha fucka! Crazy mutha fucka!"

Nothing came of the altercation, except that when Marty would walk past a group of black guys, he could swear he'd hear the phrase, "Crazy mutha fucka," every time. About a week later Marty crossed paths with Sergeant Ward again.

Andre had gotten into a fist fight with a white guy, and everyone was pointing the finger at him, as the one who started it. It was serious enough that the company commander wanted to know what happened. Andre was liable to lose his rank as sergeant, if found guilty. But Marty had witnessed the fight. He knew that Andre didn't start it. He knew that he had gotten ganged up on by a few white guys. He went to the company commander and told him what he'd seen. By him doing so, he'd saved Andre's butt. From then on, Marty was alright in his book.

Andre was from Mobile, Alabama, and he was an equipment operator like Pat. Marty had never had much association with black people, and even though he wasn't a bigot, he'd always thought them to be different. That changed for him during his time in the military. He made a lot of black friends, and Andre became a good friend. Many a night they sat up on guard duty and talked about their most personal thoughts and dreams.

Marty got to know Andre's wife Camille and daughter Sasha.

47

He became a regular at their house for cookouts and Christmas. Marty began to realize that all people were brothers and sisters, and no matter what different cultures they came from they were mostly all the same inside.

4

Another guy that Marty met was a big blonde haired, southern boy named Jerry Lee Pennebaker. He was from Leland, Mississippi and went by the nickname of Country. He played guitar and had a beautiful Martin D45 acoustic. Country always wore a cowboy hat when he was off duty, and he was also into heroin, like Marty.

Marty and the guys spent a lot of time together, drinking and chasing women. They went to bars all over the Frankfurt area, and even paid visits to the red light district, where a city block was devoted to hotels filled with prostitutes. In Germany, prostitution was legal. The whores were given regular check-ups by doctors to make sure that they stayed free of disease. Marty got to know some of the girls. They would get heroin for him and give him his fixes. It was always good to have someone else fix you, in case of an overdose. Marty made sporadic use of the heroin. He didn't want to become an addict, especially in the military.

A few months had passed, and Marty and Pat were downtown one night looking for women. Pat had started getting cozy with a girl at one of the tables, so Marty ducked out for a while. He went into one of the 'whore hotels' and started looking around. He noticed a beautiful brunette and went in to see her. As usual, she made him pay first. She told him to undress and sit on the bed. Marty obliged, and asked her to blow him first. The request seemed to annoy her, and not a minute after she began, she stopped and told him to get out.

Marty told her that it wasn't a problem. He asked her if they could just have sex. She halfheartedly agreed, and began to guide him into her. Suddenly she pushed him off and started yelling at him to leave. "Nein, gehen. Lassen Sie hier!"

Marty couldn't understand everything that she was saying, but he got the message. He got dressed and demanded that she return his money. This time he understood every word. "Fuck you! Now, get out of here!" He demanded his money again, and she called the bouncers. Two huge fellows dragged him downstairs and threw him out on the street. Marty was pissed off, and he swore that he'd, "Get that bitch, someday!" He also swore that he was finished with prostitutes.

And he would stay true to his word. "I'll never pay for sex again," he told Pat. "I can get all the pussy I want, for free!"

"It's never free," his friend replied. "You always wind up paying. One way...or another."

Marty still had a score to settle. He waited a few weeks, and then he paid one last visit to the red light district. He wasn't looking to satisfy his sexual desires though. He went upstairs to the woman's room, and asked her if he could come in. She didn't recognize him, and she waved him inside. The woman collected his money first, just as she had done before. This time Marty watched where she put it. He kept his shoes on and pushed his pants down, but didn't take them off. The woman opened her legs and said, "Kommen sie hier, bitte." Marty climbed onto her and pushed himself in. He slid in and out of her, slowly at first, and she told him to get on with it. Marty was there to teach her a lesson, and he began to slam the length of his cock in and out of her so hard, that he hurt her. She pushed him off and started yelling for the bouncers. Marty quickly pulled up his pants and went over to the drawer where she had put the money.

Inside he saw much more cash than he had paid, and he grabbed it all. She jumped up and started hitting him, and tried to hold him there. Marty pushed her back onto the bed and took off down the stairs. He passed the bouncers in the stairwell, and ran out of the building. A couple of blocks down, Marty went into a pub and ordered a beer. As he caught his breath, he counted the money. He had almost four hundred marks, which was well over one hundred dollars. Marty was quite happy with himself, and bragged to Pat later that he'd robbed a whorehouse. Pat was proud of him.

5

When the guys got bored around town, they would take leave time and hit the road. By bus or train, they would travel to the different countries that surrounded Germany. They partied in France, and smoked dope in the pubs of Amsterdam. In the Alps of Switzerland, they skied down the side of a mountain, stopping at a chalet to eat lunch, before winding down the rest of the way to the bottom, in time for supper. One of their craziest trips was when they went to Mataró, Spain.

The resort that they stayed at featured a topless beach. At first, they couldn't take their eyes off of the girls. But by the next day they had gotten used to it, and it was no big deal. All three guys hooked up with beautiful girls. Marty met a girl from Portugal named Marisa. Pat and Country hit it off with a couple of British girls named Patti and Chrissi. They had hoped to meet Spanish girls, but they were in an area filled with tourists and there weren't many local girls that hung out at the clubs. Still, the girls made for some fun days and warm nights, making love on the moonlit beach.

The third night they were there, they all went into a pub called 'The Piccadilly.' At first the place was empty, and they had a good time dancing and playing pool. Patti and Chrissi were like a comedy team. They told one joke after another, and Marty thought they had the dirtiest mouth's for women that he had ever heard. After a few hours in the place, they all started getting drunk.

Soon the pub began to fill up with people. Most of which were a group of weightlifters, who after a while started trying to dance with Marty and Pat. Country was passed out drunk by this time, and Chrissi was trying to wake him up. Marisa found out that the men were homosexuals, and that these muscle boys wanted some action.

Marty and Pat talked it over, and in their drunken wisdom decided to give them some. Pat proceeded to clobber a guy over the head with a beer bottle. Marty swung a pool stick, and it cracked in half against another guy's chest. Chairs started flying, and so did the punches. Country woke up and got punched in the mouth before he even knew what was going on. Marty was getting crushed by a couple of huge guys, when the cops came in and started busting heads.

Somehow, the three friends and their girls managed to crawl out of the melee and get away. They ran down the sidewalk, and into another club. "I think I knocked that one guy's teeth out!" Pat cackled, as they all laughed, recounting the events. But soon, Marisa told

Marty, "I've had enough of this," and they went for a walk.

The two of them sauntered down to the beach, holding hands and enjoying the moonlit night. They headed for the waters edge, and Marisa turned to Marty and kissed him. He pushed his tongue into her mouth, and she breathlessly returned the favor.

Marty's hands moved down to her bum, and she pushed him away. His surprise turned to arousal, as she stripped off her clothes and ran into the water. "C'mon in!" she teased. He undressed and joined her. They frolicked in the waves, as the tide came in, and then they went back up to continue were they left off.

Marisa was a beautiful girl with long blond hair and perfect breasts. Marty had noticed that even her pubic hair was light blond. His penis began to stiffen, and she noticed that. She reached down and began to stroke him, and they knelt down in the sand. His dick throbbed in her hand, and he knew that he had to get inside of her, before he came.

She laid on her back and spread her legs, inviting him. Marty took his time, slowly kissing his way down from her neck and shoulders, and over her peaks and valleys. He suckled her nipples and then continued downward to her nether regions. He pushed his fingers, and then his tongue into her pussy. He could taste the sand on her glistening flower, and he licked it off. He grazed his tongue over her clitoris, and she quivered at his touch.

Marisa's body began to undulate beneath him. "You're going to make me cum," she sighed. She wriggled away from him and got on her hands and knees. "Go ahead and fuck me," she teased. "I know you want to." Marty hadn't planned on needing permission, but when she wagged her behind at him, he knew he never had to ask.

He entered her, barely giving her the head of his cock. He began to tease her by pulling in and out and rubbing himself on her clit. She reached down and held it against herself and began to moan with delight. She was waiting for just the right moment to guide him back into her when she lost her balance and fell onto the sand.

She quickly propped herself back up and told Marty to let her have it. This time, he thrust himself into her with long rhythmic strokes that sent her pleasure zone into the stratosphere. She was beginning to cum, and Marty felt her clench tight around him. The sensation was all he could take. His semen shot up his shaft like a rocket, and they came together, moaning like a couple of coyotes in heat.

When they looked up, they noticed that a small group of people had gathered on the sidewalk above the beach, and had been watching them. As Marty and Marisa stood up and began to dress, the spectators started to applaud them.

A little embarrassed at first, the two lovers laughed, as they ran up to the street. Someone offered them a bottle of wine, which they took with them to their room. They finished the wine, and then they made love, until the sun came up. Only then, falling asleep in each others arms.

6

It was a beautiful summer evening, and Marty and the guys were in the middle of another night of carousing in the Sachsenhausen. They were in a place called 'The Irish Pub', guzzling Guinness beer, while a jazz record wafted from the sound system. Marty had just taken a gulp of his beer when he noticed a gorgeous blond haired woman coming through the doorway. He recognized her immediately, and he couldn't believe his eyes at first. It was Claudia, the girl he'd met on the plane coming over.

Claudia walked over to the bar and ordered a drink. Some friends came over to her, and they began to chat. Marty knew he couldn't let his chance to see her again, slip away. After a few minutes, Claudia's friends left her at the bar. She started to look around the room, and Marty made eye contact with her. He got up and went over to her and said hello. She didn't seem to recognize him at first, so he told her his name and reminded her of their meeting on the plane. "Ah, yes!" she said, "I remember now. Sorry about that."

"Hey, that's alright," he assured her. "Would you like to sit with me? What have you been up to lately? It's amazing we actually bumped into each other again!"

Claudia agreed to sit with Marty. "What do you mean when you say...bumped into each other?" she asked.

"Well...you know. Just that we met again. I mean, what were the chances of that."

What were the chances, indeed. Marty was mesmerized. They drank their beer, and he offered her a cigarette. He lit it for her and asked what her plans were for the evening. Claudia blew her cigarette smoke into the air, and told him that she had been invited to a friend's birthday party. Marty wanted to get into Claudia's pants in the worst way possible. He didn't want to let her go. He hoped that she would invite him along, but after a few minutes she told him that she had to go. He walked outside with her and told her that he hoped to see her again. To his surprise, she gave him a long and passionate kiss, pushing her tongue into his mouth. "I'll be seeing you," she told him, and then she turned and walked away.

Marty had been sitting there drowning his sorrows, when about a half an hour later, Claudia came back into the pub. She walked up to him and said, "Quickly...put your arms around me and pretend that you are my boyfriend!" He gladly did as she asked. She continued, "A man will be coming in here and I want to get rid of him!"

She began to kiss him, and once more her tongue darted into his mouth. As they embraced, he felt his cock begin to stiffen, and he pulled back, embarrassed that she would feel it. "No, I want to feel you getting aroused," she scolded and pulled him back to her.

Marty didn't see any guy come in, and he wondered what he was letting himself in for. He didn't care. He wanted Claudia, and he was willing to play any kind of game she came up with. "Maybe this is how she gets her kicks," he thought.

"Do you want to go to my place?" she asked. He told her that there was nothing he would like more. They left the pub and walked for several blocks, until they came to her apartment.

Once inside Claudia told Marty to put on some music. "Get comfy...I'll be right back," she assured him, as she went into her bedroom. Marty pinched himself to make sure that it wasn't a dream. A few minutes later, she returned wearing nothing but her panties. They snuggled up on the couch and began to kiss. "Why don't you make yourself comfortable," she cooed and started to undo Marty's pants. "I don't want to be the only one who is undressed here."

He helped her out and was quickly down to his boxers. Again, they began to kiss, and Marty gently caressed Claudia's breasts, squeezing her pink nipples between his fingertips. Her breath began to quicken, and she slid her hand into his shorts. He brushed his hand down her belly and over the soft skin of her inner thighs. He pressed his fingers against her panties, and could feel the dampness of her natural eagerness.

Marty pulled her panties aside and slid his fingers into her vagina. Claudia sighed and kissed him, even harder. She pulled his cock through the fly of his shorts and pushed him back on the couch. Pulling her panties aside, she slid down on top of him. She began to slowly glide up and down Marty's shaft. She leaned down to kiss him, and he pushed his tongue into her mouth. As their lovemaking became more intense, Claudia arched back and started to moan. Marty pushed his length in and out of her. He knew that she was about to cum and it pushed him over the edge. The chance meeting with this exciting woman, and the events of their encounter had really turned him on. After he'd finished, he could swear that it was the longest orgasm he'd ever had.

Claudia asked Marty if he'd like to have a bubble bath with her. "That sounds great," he replied. He washed her feet, and she washed his back. They washed each others faces, and when Marty began to wash her vagina, he couldn't resist. He fingered her, until she came.

When they'd finished their bath, they dried each other off and climbed into bed. They talked for a while, and then Claudia began to suck his cock. As Marty watched, he thought about how beautiful she was and felt like he was falling in love. They made love again and fell asleep in each others arms.

The next day they went sightseeing and shopping. Claudia bought a big floppy hat and a pair of boots. Marty bought a few record albums. They had lunch, and afterward they stopped for some ice cream.

On the train ride back to her place, the light grew dim, as the sun began to hide behind the buildings and trees along the way. As the shadows danced around them, Claudia opened Marty's fly and lowered her panties to her thighs. They snuggled close together and she nestled her bum against his lap. They made love, as the other passengers stared out the window, possibly thinking about their busy lives, or their own lover, waiting for them at home.

In the morning Marty had to leave. He didn't want to give up the heaven that he'd been in for the past day and a half. Claudia assured him that they would see each other again. She wrote down her phone number and added, 'hugs and kisses'.

For the next two weeks Headquarters Company was training in the field. The whole time, all Marty could think about was Claudia. He bragged about her to the guys, and Andre said that maybe some night they could come over for dinner. When Marty got back to Frankfurt, the first thing he did was call her. To his surprise, a guy with an American voice answered the phone. He thought that he had the wrong number, and he hung up. He dialed again and the same man answered. Marty used a German accent, and asked to speak to Claudia. "She isn't here, right now," the guy replied. "Can I take a message?"

Marty's heart sank. "Who is this guy?" he wondered to himself. "No thank you," he said and hung up the phone. He couldn't believe it. "Was this guy her boyfriend...her husband?" Marty fretted over it to the point of paranoia. Why hadn't he noticed any sign of a man's belongings in her apartment. "Did she have two homes...two lives? Was any of it even real?" Marty called her again a couple days later. This time, she answered. "What's going on!" he demanded. "Who was that guy?"

"I can't talk now," she replied.

"I thought we had something good going!" he cried.

"Oh, grow up!" she said angrily. "He's just a guy! I like to be spontaneous, I like to have affairs! It was just a fling Marty! Leave it like that!"

"Can I see you again?"

"No Marty...it's best you don't call me again, please!" She hung up the phone.

Marty pined over her for a couple of weeks, and then he threw her phone number away. He found out the hard way that a woman could play games too. That if you were going to dish it out, you had to learn to take it. But Marty needn't have worried. He didn't know it yet, but his life was about to take a turn that would make him forget all about Claudia.

7

Life in the Army barracks was pretty simple. Every now and then, the first sergeant would inspect the rooms, but for the most part it was fairly laid back. Marty and the guys would sit around and drink beer, while they listened to records and played cards. Many nights they would play guitars and sing along. Pat played guitar, and Marty blew his harmonica. Country would sit there playing his Martin, in his underwear and a cowboy hat. Marty was getting to be fairly good on guitar, too. They mostly played country western and blues numbers.

If they felt like it, they could mosey on down to the 'Enlisted Club' that was there on the post. They could get as drunk as they pleased, and wouldn't have far to stagger back to their bed. It was in the midst of such an evening, when Marty noticed a new bartender was serving drinks. "I think I need another beer," he said, and he left his friends at the table. He sauntered over to her and introduced himself.

She smiled and told him that her name was Cherilyn. She was friendly and easy to talk to. He stayed at the bar, and they talked the evening away.

Cherilyn Stover was from Palo Alto, California. Her parents had been in the Army at the beginning of the Korean War. Her father was a black man named Jim Haynes. Her mother was a white woman named Betty Johnson. They were both assigned to the same medical unit—he was a surgeon and she was a nurse. They'd had a love affair while they were there, and Betty had become pregnant. They had planned to get married, but Jim was killed by sniper fire.

Betty was processed out of the military, and six months later, she gave birth to Cherilyn. They moved to Palo Alto, and that's where Cherilyn grew up. Her mother eventually met and married another man, had another daughter, and then divorced the guy.

Marty told Cherilyn he was sorry about her dad. "So...Cherilyn, how'd you end up in this place?" The answer that she gave wasn't anything like what he had hoped to hear.

Cherilyn and a guy named Steve Stover had been high school sweethearts, even though they'd mostly kept it a secret. Steve was white, and in the sixties, interracial relationships were still severely frowned upon. It was a sad fact, but one that young people were trying to change. When Steve was drafted into the Army and being sent to boot camp, he asked Cherilyn if she would marry him. She agreed, but only if they did it as soon as he returned. About three months later, they were hitched. A week after that, they were in Frankfurt.

Things went well at first. They were placed in government housing, and a happy Cherilyn had fun decorating their new apartment. They made friends with other couples and took turns playing cards at each others homes. But after a while, the card parties turned into drunken binges for Steve. He began to change, and soon, he became abusive towards Cherilyn. Things only got worse between the two of them. When she had taken one beating too many, she moved out of the apartment, and in with some friends. Steve went there one night and tried to talk her into coming back. She told him that they were finished. He said he'd never give her a divorce. She told him, that as soon as she'd made enough money, she would buy a plane ticket and fly back to California. A month later, Steve got busted with hashish and was on his way to being kicked out of the Army—dishonorably of course.

"And that is how I came to be in this place," Cherilyn finished sarcastically. And then she laughed and said, "Let me buy you a beer, Marty. You look like you need one, after hearing all that."

Marty gladly took her up on it. Then, he asked her, "So...when you get the money...you're gonna go, huh?"

"That's the plan."

"Nothing can change your mind?"

"Well...let's just say it would have to be somethin', pretty darn good."

8

Pat noticed that Marty was spending a lot of time in the 'Enlisted Club', lately. "C'mon downtown with us tonight, Marty. You haven't been out for weeks now. What's in that club that you like so much?"

"Aw, you know," Marty replied.

"No, I don't know," Pat said gruffly. "Don't tell me you're getting puss whopped by that twat!"

Marty was spending less time with the guys. He and Cherilyn had become friends, and he had been with her almost every day. She had a car, and they went for long drives in the country. She introduced him to her friend Veronica and her husband Phil. Phil was a squad leader in 'Charlie' company, at Camp Eschborn.

Now, Marty was playing partners at the card games, and he was getting used to having Cherilyn by his side. But he was worried about her husband Steve, and he figured that she was going to leave sooner or later anyway.

It was late one evening, and Marty had stuck around the club, as he'd done most nights, waiting for Cherilyn to close up. He helped her pick up glasses, and they talked, as she wiped down the tables. She asked him if he wanted to go shopping with her in the morning. "I need to get a decent jacket," she said. "It's getting colder and winter's coming."

"You keep spending all your money, and you're never gonna get that plane ticket."

Cherilyn stopped wiping and turned towards him. "Do you want to go with me, or not?" She looked into his eyes, and right then he realized that she didn't want to go anywhere.

Marty pulled her to him, and as they began to kiss, he felt a warm sensation rush through him, that started at his toes and went straight to his head. His heart began to pound in his chest, and within seconds, his dick became harder than a Chinese puzzle. He lifted her sweater, and she let him pull it off of her. Cherilyn removed her bra and dropped it on the floor. As he sucked her nipples, she moaned and begged him to take his pants off. He obliged her request, and she feverishly helped him tug them down.

She lowered her skirt and panties, kicking them aside. He lifted her onto the table and pushed his cock inside of her. Cherilyn leaned back, hands on the table, and let Marty give it to her fast and hard. He could feel his loins beginning to burn inside of him. She began to cum, and she lurched forward hanging on to his shoulders, as her body shuddered in ecstasy. Marty let himself go, his semen completely filling her. They kissed each other tenderly, as their breath slowly returned. "I don't think I'll be needin' a plane ticket," she whimpered contently.

They got dressed and Cherilyn finished closing up. She turned out the lights, and they stepped outside. As she locked the door, she realized that she hadn't wiped the table where they had just made love. They laughed at the thought, that the next day—where her ass and his semen had been—someone would be drinking beer and eating french fries.

Cherilyn's husband Steve had been under restriction to post because of his drug bust, and their government apartment was, for the time being, unoccupied. She suggested to Marty that they move in together, until the Army got around to processing Steve out of there. Marty was apprehensive, but he agreed, and they moved in that night. Cherilyn had kept her set of keys, and as she turned the lock, Marty crossed his fingers. This was the beginning of something serious. It was the first time that he had lived with a woman, and he had high hopes for what the future might bring. He had no ida of the tempestuous time that lay ahead for both of them.

9

Marty was dreaming. He and a nurse were having sex on a bed in the center of a hospital emergency room. Suddenly, the door swung open. A line of naked chorus girls danced into the room, around the bed, and back out the door. The scene began to fade, and Marty awoke from his dream. He had an erection, and Cherilyn was sucking it. She stopped for a second and smiled at him. "Time for breakfast," she giggled. Marty pulled her to him and pushed his tongue into her mouth. She slid down on top of him, and they began to make love.

When they were finished, Cherilyn got up and went to make them something to eat. Marty laid there and wondered what he had gotten himself into. Cherilyn—as it turned out—was quite the little nympho. No matter how much he gave her, it was never enough. Her insatiable needs were leaving Marty drained. They couldn't drive to the supermarket without her having to suck him off. She blew him in the men's room at the concert hall. When they went to the club, she'd want fucked in the car—before they went inside.

They hadn't been together for three weeks, and Marty was starting to get cold feet. Cherilyn wasn't even legally separated from Steve, and that worried Marty. He could get kicked out of the Army for adultery. When they were together in the car, she'd let Marty drive. But he didn't have a license to drive in Germany, and in the military any little screw up could get you into big trouble.

Just as he was thinking that he didn't need it, he heard someone come in the apartment door. It was a man, and Marty knew it was Steve. He jumped out of bed and started to get dressed. He could hear them starting to argue. Steve came down the hall, and into the bedroom. He had Marty's boots, and he said, "I guess these would be yours." Marty couldn't answer—his stomach was in his throat. Steve threw the shoes onto the bed and went back out into the kitchen. Marty thought that he'd seen this in a movie, once. He was afraid something like this was going to happen. But he couldn't believe that it really did. He felt like a heel, and he just wanted to get out of there. He grabbed his boots and walked down the hall. Steve was staring out the living room window, and Marty went for the door. "Don't you go, Marty!" Cherilyn cried. "Steve is the one that's leaving!"

Marty looked into her eyes and watched a tear run down her cheek. He said, "I'll see ya, baby," and then he opened the door and left.

When the evening formation broke up the next day, Cherilyn

was waiting for Marty. She told him that Steve was being sent back home in a couple of days. He had come back to the apartment to pack his stuff. Marty didn't say anything, so she went on. "The Army is going to pay for my plane ticket, too. I gotta let 'em know by noon tomorrow." Marty thought for a minute, and then he held Cherilyn tight in his arms. He kissed her, and then he backed away from her. "I think you better take 'em up on it," he said. Then he turned and went inside.

In his room, Marty banged his head against the wall. He didn't really want Cherilyn to go, but he was scared of the commitment he'd have to make if she stayed. "It's better this way," he thought. He took a shower, and then he went down to the club and grabbed a six pack. He was glad Cherilyn wasn't there. He decided to take a walk in the wooded area that was behind the post. After a while, he came upon a lookout tower, and he climbed up inside.

Marty cracked open a beer and watched, as the sun began to set. He was on his third beer, when he noticed someone coming down the path. "Hey there, mister ranger," she chuckled. "What'cha doin' up there?"

"Why don't you come up and see for yourself?" he sighed. Cherilyn started climbing, and when she reached the top, Marty pulled her up. "How'd you know I was here? Wait...don't tell me, a little birdie told you...right?"

"Actually, it was your buddy, Pat."

"Well, how about that," he thought.

Marty gave her a beer, and they sat down and watched the sunset together.

10

Not only was Cherilyn horny, but she was crazy too. There was no limit, to the chances that she was willing to take to be with Marty. Stunts, like climbing the fire escape to his second floor room in the barracks, to make love with him, were nothing compared to what she was really capable of.

One evening, they had gone to dinner with Andre and Camille. They had just finished ordering their meals, and Andre was pouring the wine. Cherilyn took Marty's hand under the table and slid it up her thigh, and under her skirt. He was surprised to realize that she wasn't wearing any panties. She began to rub his fingers on her vagina, and when she slipped them inside of herself, Andre and Camille could see that she was becoming visibly aroused.

The two exhibitionists excused themselves and went out to their car. They fucked for a half an hour, and Marty was so turned on that he came twice without stopping. When they returned to their seats, they continued the evening with their friends, as if nothing unusual had happened.

Marty decided that he and Cherilyn needed to find and apartment. Luckily, a guy in his squad named Gary McDowell offered to share his place with them. In a short while, Marty's military hitch would be over, and they gladly took him up on it. The two lovers lived in unmarried bliss for the next several months.

Pat's time in the military was also coming to an end. The way he saw things, it was time for him and Marty to go out with a bang. It just so happened that his birthday had come up, and he insisted that Marty come out with him. To Pat's disappointment, Cherilyn insisted on coming along. The place they chose was a huge dancehall, with a second floor balcony that stretched completely around the room. The gang found seats at a table along the railing with a clear view of the floor below.

Cherilyn began to sense the guys had been there before. Her fears were confirmed when they began to assemble a long hose made from straws, which they lowered into the beer mugs on the tables below. She almost couldn't believe her eyes as they siphoned the liquid up through the makeshift hoses, and into their mouths. The best part, was the bewildered looks on the face's of the people, when they came back from dancing and found their mugs empty.

Everyone was getting drunk. Marty decided to make a toast in Pat's honor, and when the people at the next table didn't join in, he took exception. "Hey! Didn't you hear! It's Pat's birthday...how about a little respect!"

"Yeah, yeah," they responded halfheartedly. "Hooray for your friend."

Cherilyn said, "Marty, why don't you sit down."

"How do you like this, Pat? How about this! I said...it's my friend's birthday, you assholes!"

"Hey, fuck you, man!" One of the guys stood up, and Marty threw his beer mug at him. He ducked, and the mug shattered against the wall above them, spraying glass and beer everywhere. A brawl ensued, and Pat and Country jumped in. Even Cherilyn was throwing punches. As usual, Marty was at the bottom of the pile. Soon the Polizei arrived and started cracking heads.

Cherilyn pulled Marty out from the abyss, and they took off, leaving their coats and their buddies behind. They didn't stop running until they got to the train station, both of them out of breath. Marty started to laugh, and Cherilyn became enraged. She slapped him in the mouth and shoved him into the bushes. "You idiot! You stupid, fucking jerk! What the hell is wrong with you!" Marty got up, and she tried to shove him again. This time he grabbed her and pulled her down with him, and in doing so, he ripped her blouse half off of her.

"Aw, Fuck...now, look what you did!" she cried. "Look at this! I'm through with this bullshit...I've had it! I went through this shit with Steve...and I ain't gonna go through it again!"

Marty felt bad for her. He told her he was sorry and gave her his sweater. The two of them went back to their car, and they drove home. Pat and Country didn't have it so easy. The Polizei had turned them over to the military police, and they spent the night in the cooler.

11

A few weeks later, a very sad thing happened. Country had been downtown shooting heroin by himself. He was found in a bathroom stall, unconscious and the needle still in his arm. By the time the ambulance reached him, he was dead. Everyone was devastated. To Marty, it was like losing a brother. As he and Pat packed Country's personal belongings, he picked up the Martin and began to strum a few chords. "Remember what he told you," Pat said. "That if anything ever happened, he wanted you to have it." Marty remembered, and for a long time after when he played that guitar, it brought a tear to his eye.

Country's death made Marty think about his own life. He realized that it wasn't so bad, and he vowed to make the most of it. He swore off heroin and told Cherilyn that if she divorced Steve, he'd marry her. It had taken a while, but Marty finally told her he loved her. "I love you too, Marty!" she cried, as happy as could be. "I will marry you!"

It was New Year's Eve, and Marty and Cherilyn had a week left in Germany. They had picked Andre and Camille up and were out for the night's revelry. The Germans celebrated the coming of the new year with fireworks, and there was plenty of drinking to be done. Pat had already gone home, and time was growing short for the four friends. They had almost reached their destination when Cherilyn told Marty that she didn't feel well. She had an upset stomach, and she felt like she was going to puke. Camille said, "Well, that stinks!"

"Are you sure?" Marty asked her.

"Yes, I'm sure!" she insisted.

"Oh well, I guess we'll drop you guys off and go home," he told Andre. "Unless, you wanna come back with us."

Before Andre could answer, Cherilyn said that she just wanted to go to bed. They told Marty to drop them off, and they got out at Sachsenhausen. "Hope you're alright," Camille said to Cherilyn.

"Thanks, you guys. Have a happy New Year's," she replied.

Andre said, "Same to you," and he shook Marty's hand.

When they got home, Cherilyn said that she was starting to feel better. "There's still time to go back out," Marty coaxed.

"No...I just want you all to myself," she cooed mischievously. She went into the bedroom and came back a few minutes later, draped in a blanket. Standing in front of Marty, she let it drop to the floor, revealing her gorgeous naked body. "You weren't sick at all...were you," he scolded.

"Now, Marty...be nice," she pouted and began to unzip his pants. She climbed on top of him, and as they made love, Marty couldn't think of a better way to spend the evening. A new year was starting, and it was the beginning of a new life for him and Cherilyn. They both began to cum at the stroke of midnight, and through their window they could see fireworks going off over Frankfurt, as their orgasm's swept through their bodies.

PART THREE

1

When they stepped off the plane at JFK airport, the first thing Marty did was get on his hands and knees and kiss the ground. He was glad to be back on American soil. "Oh, Marty... Get up!" Cherilyn laughed. She was happy to be home too. At least, almost home. They still had two more flights to take until they reached Palo Alto.

Cherilyn had missed her mother, and the first thing she wanted to do was get home to see her. The second thing she wanted to do was file for divorce from Steve. They boarded their connecting flight, and about five hours later they were in L.A. The Los Angeles airport was huge. It took them almost forty minutes to get to the gate for their commuter flight to Palo Alto. On the way, the plane hit some turbulence, and actually fell for several seconds. The two travelers were relieved when they were on the ground, for good.

Cherilyn's Uncle Albert met them at the airport. They piled

their stuff into his station wagon, and made it home in a half hour. Uncle Albert told them that they were invited to his place for steaks on the grill the next day. It was good to be back in America. The California air agreed with Marty. It felt different—lighter maybe— and calm. And the people seemed more laid back. It didn't take long for him to feel the connection with the west coast's dreamy romanticism.

Cherilyn's mother was glad to see her, and she liked Marty right away. She served sandwiches to tide them over, until dinner time. Her sister Cindy wasn't as easy to win over. She was a couple of years younger than Cherilyn—barely out of high school—and very hot. But she liked Steve and blamed Marty for pushing Cherilyn away from him. As they sat in the living room, Cindy shot Marty an icy look. He could hear Betty in the kitchen telling Cherilyn that Steve had met someone else. She kept up her snippy attitude the rest of the evening, and really never warmed up to Marty at all.

The next day, Marty met Aunt Alice and Cousin Larry, and a gang of other relatives. His steak was so big it filled up his whole plate. Uncle Albert jokingly advised him to use two. They had a great time and everyone made him feel like part of the family. Even Cindy did. She was like a snotty kid sister who couldn't help but make wisecracks. Marty liked her. So much that when he caught her behind the garage smoking pot, he promised not to tell. "Your secret's safe with me," he told her, as he took a drag, himself.

Later that night, Marty and Cherilyn made love in the

backyard, under the stars. In the moonlight, she looked like an angel. He thought about how people on the east coast say that California is the Devil's playground. But as he watched Cherilyn glide up and down his shaft, he could swear that he'd finally reached heaven.

Cherilyn contacted a lawyer about filing for a divorce against Steve, on grounds of physical abuse. A few days later, the lawyer contacted her and informed her that Steve had beaten her to the punch, claiming that she had committed adultery. He advised her that she could petition her own claim, or agree with his. The turn of events knocked the wind out of her sails. She had wanted to be the one who hammered Steve. Now, what was the use. A week later, she signed the papers—in essence admitting adultery—giving Steve his divorce. When they stepped outside the lawyer's office, she spun into Marty's arms and broke down.

"I feel like such a fool."

"Yeah, but you're my little fool," he assured her.

Cherilyn wiped her eyes and smiled. "I am," she laughed, "and don't forget it."

For the next week Cherilyn showed Marty around. They went into San Francisco, and to Haight-Ashbury. They saw a few hippies and everything was cool, but it wasn't the same anymore. All of the rock bands had moved out of town. Still, it was a beautiful city. They went to a few shows at the famous concert venues around the city, and saw a couple of their favorite bands.

They were shopping one afternoon, and Marty was getting

bored, as Cherilyn went from store to store trying on clothes. He suggested that they stop for lunch. They hit a burger joint, and afterwards went into a department store. Marty found a few things he liked and went into a fitting room to try them on.

He had barely gotten his pants off, when suddenly, Cherilyn appeared in the room. "Aah, haa!" she laughed mischievously. "I've caught you with your pants down!" She undid her jeans and let them drop to her ankles. "Let me join you," she cooed, as she seductively wriggled her panties down. Cherilyn pulled Marty close and began to fondle his crotch. His nervousness dissolved, as his cock began to stiffen in her hands. "Do me right here," she teased.

She put her hands against the wall and arched her bum into the air, beckoning him. He got behind her, and slowly pushed the length of his shaft into her opening. "See how fast you can make me cum," she dared. Marty slid in and out of her a few times, and then pulled back to tease her. "Oh, C'mon Marty...just let me have it!" This time he gave her what she wanted, and as he glided in and out of her, she started to moan. "SSSHHH!" he scolded. "We'll get caught!"

Cherilyn laughed breathlessly, and Marty began to thrust into her faster and harder. He felt himself beginning to cum and thought that she wasn't going to make it. But seconds later, she was there, and when she moaned again, Marty cupped his hand over her mouth. They tried to keep a straight face, as they came out together, and a saleswoman eyed them suspiciously. They broke up with laughter, and the saleswoman just shrugged her shoulders with a look of wonder.

Marty had done some shopping of his own. That evening, as he and Cherilyn sat on the front steps, he gave her an engagement ring, and he officially proposed. He told her that he thought that the month of May was a good time to get married, because it was a time when everything came to life. She agreed, and happily said yes.

2

Marty called his Aunt Nina in Pittsburgh to ask for Liz's phone number. She told him that Uncle Wilbur died the December before last. Marty never knew. He hadn't contacted anyone in his family the whole time he was overseas. He told her that he was sorry, and maybe he'd see her soon. But he had no intentions of going home. She gave him Liz's number, and they said goodbye.

He called Liz, and told her he was in Palo Alto. She told him about her dad, and he said he was sorry, and that her mom had told him. After a little chit-chat, she gave him her address. That evening, Marty and Cherilyn went to visit Liz. When they arrived, she was surprised to see Cherilyn. Marty hadn't told her about them. When he told Liz they were engaged to be married, Cherilyn could see the disappointment in her eyes. Marty told her again, that he was sorry about her dad. She thanked him and said, "It's a curse. A curse from the old country on the men in our family."

"You know, I've thought the same thing," he told her.

Cherilyn looked at both of them and said, "Okay guys... you're freaking me out."

Liz said, "Sorry darlin'...hey, who wants to smoke a joint?"

Marty's eyes lit up, and he started to say, "We..." when Cherilyn cut him off. "Thanks anyway, Liz, but we aren't really into that stuff."

Marty said, "Huh? Wait a minute. There ain't nothin' wrong with a little bit of pot."

This time it was Liz, who noticed the disappointment in Cherilyn's eyes. "Ohh...you know what...I'm sorry. I just remembered that I smoked my last bit of weed this morning. Oh well..."

Marty shrugged. "Hey, that's alright. Sooo...what have you been up to?"

Liz told them that she had started to take classes in engineering, but dropped out after a few months. She'd decided to go to nursing school instead. When she graduated, she took a job in a hospital, but didn't like working shifts. Then, she landed a job as a medical assistant in a doctor's office. "Pays the rent," she laughed.

Then she asked, "What are you looking for, Marty? I can give Uncle Josh a call down there in Albuquerque. He can give you a job in the rail yard. You'd make big bucks. That's if you and Cherilyn would be willing to go there."

3

Marty and Cherilyn bought a used Chevy van and loaded their
belongings into it. They said goodbye to Betty and Cindy and headed
for New Mexico. They had gotten a late start, and stayed in Flagstaff,
Arizona overnight. By the next evening they were pulling into Uncle
Josh's driveway. Josh Millen was Liz's mom's brother. He was a
bachelor, and had been living in New Mexico for most of his life. He
was a big burly man, whose laugh echoed halfway across the
neighborhood.

Uncle Josh was high up in the chain of command at the rail
yard. He got Marty a job on the 'Track Gang', which was a
maintenance crew. He told him he could start Monday. "Just do a
good job, and I'll help ya out with anything," he said. Marty was
grateful. He let them stay at his place for a few days, until they found
an apartment. A few days was all they needed. They found a trailer

for rent by Friday, and they moved in over the weekend. It took them a while to furnish it, and make it feel like home. But this time, as Cherilyn decorated, she really felt like everything was going to be alright.

A couple of weeks after they'd been there, Marty called Liz to thank her for the connection with Uncle Josh. He told her that it was going great, and he hoped that they would stay in touch. She said that she was happy for him, and that she hoped for the same. As he was saying goodbye, he said, "Take it easy, Cuz."

Liz told him, "Same to you...and Marty...don't ever call me Cuz, again."

Wade Benson worked with Marty on the track gang. They got along well, and after a month they had become pretty good friends. It was a Friday, and Wade invited Marty to bring Cherilyn over to the house for a barbecue, "and meet the wife."

When Marty got home, he told Cherilyn, and she agreed that it would be nice to start meeting people. She was a little apprehensive though, considering she hadn't been thrilled with Marty's taste in friends, up to this point. They both got ready, and then they drove over to meet their new friends, who as it turned out, only lived a few blocks away. When they arrived, Wade came out of the house to greet them. He was a tall sandy haired fellow with a smile from ear to ear. He offered his hand to Cherilyn, and Marty introduced them. "The wife's waitin' in the back," he said. "Let's go get a beer." They followed him to the back patio. "Marty...Cherilyn...this is my wife,

Rowena."

"Pleased to make your acquaintance," she said. "How about a couple of beers."

Marty was impressed. Rowena was an extremely gorgeous girl, and she was clearly of oriental descent. But the thing that really floored him, was that she spoke with a New York accent. She gave them their beers, and they all settled down to telling their stories.

The Benson's seemed like the most unlikely couple that you'd ever see. Wade was from San Antonio—the son of ranchers. Rowena was from the Bronx in New York city. She was the daughter of a white American father and a Japanese mother, who met at the end of the second world war. Sakura Kuro was a government detainee during the war, and Ron Huxley was a pencil pusher for the defense department. He fell in love with her, and they married, so she could gain her U.S. citizenship. When a baby came along, Ron insisted they name her Rowena, after his favorite aunt from Long Island. The Huxley's eventually divorced, and Rowena stayed with her mother in New York. They ran a Japanese restaurant, and that's where she met Wade, when he and some buddies made a trip to the 'Big Apple'.

Wade and Rowena did have a few things in common. They both seemed to like beer, and after dinner, Marty and Cherilyn found out that they loved cocaine. Cherilyn passed when they offered them some, but Marty heartily accepted, pissing her off. They also told them that they were musicians. They both played guitar and keyboards, and Rowena was in an all girl band called 'The Dishes'.

They played at a bar she worked at called 'The Tumbleweed' and a few other places in town. Wade had been in a few bands, and he was a songwriter. Marty told them that he played guitar and harmonica. They all agreed that they would have to get together and jam.

When they got home, Cherilyn was still mad at Marty for snorting cocaine. "I don't know if I like them," she said. "And that Rowena...she looked at me funny, all night long."

Marty told her, "You have gotta loosen up, sweetheart. You're too uptight. We're young...live a little."

"Maybe you're right, Marty. Maybe I will." But she wasn't sure.

The next day Rowena called and offered to get Cherilyn a job at 'The Tumbleweed'. That morning someone had quit, and they needed her to start that night, if she was willing to. She talked it over with Marty, and he said, "Go for it."

She called Rowena back. "I'll take it," she said gladly. "Thanks a bunch."

"No problem, darlin'. I'll pick you up at four, and we'll go down there and get you started."

Cherilyn hung up the phone and told Marty, "Ya know, maybe Rowena ain't so bad, after all."

4

With Cherilyn at work, Marty had resigned himself to an
evening alone. He cracked open a beer and began to play his guitar.
He was about to make himself something to eat, when the phone rang.
It was Rowena. "Do ya wanna come over and be with me and Wade?"

"Well, it's just gonna be me."

"Oh, yeah," she said, "That's alright. Come on over, anyway."

Marty figured they'd sit around and do some blow, and it would
also be a good chance for them to do some playing. "I'll bring my
guitar," he suggested.

"Oh, sure...that's cool. Bring it along."

When Marty got to their house, Wade had lines on the mirror
and a cold beer ready. They began to pick a few tunes. He showed
Marty some of his songs, and soon a few things started to click.
Rowena seemed disinterested, and after a while she left the two

collaborators to themselves. She returned a half an hour later, wearing only a flannel shirt and panties. The shirt was completely unbuttoned, exposing her bare breasts. "Let's get comfortable," she cooed, and she began to unbutton Marty's pants. Marty looked at Wade, and he just smiled. "Rowena wants to give me the best blow job ever, and she wants fucked while she does it."

Marty quickly realized that this had been planned. Wade and Rowena were swingers. Rowena bit her lip and stared intently at Marty's dick, as she stroked him to attention. "C'mon, guys...let's get naked," she ordered. They undressed, and she began to suck on Wade's cock. She arched her behind into the air, and Marty could see by her glistening vulva, that she was inviting him, eagerly. His penis instantly began to throb, but first, he wanted to taste Rowena's pussy. He got between her legs and ran his tongue up her thigh, and into her opening. "Marty...I want you inside of me!" she panted. He knelt behind her, and she guided him into her aching wound. She moaned, as her lips moved up and down Wade's shaft. Marty began to thrust his length in and out of her, and in minutes he was about to cum. Wade couldn't hold back, and he went off like a cannon. Rowena easily took every bit of his gurgling eruption, and soon she could feel her own climax beginning to consume her. "Ooh, Marty...good boy!" she moaned, and once sated, she turned around and sucked him dry.

Rowena excused herself, while the guys drank a beer. They talked about finding some other players and starting a band. After a while, she came back into the room and said slyly, "Cherilyn wants to talk to you, Marty. It's in the bedroom." His heart began to pound, as he picked up the phone.

"Cherilyn...sweetheart," he stammered. "Everything go good at work tonight?"

"I don't care what kind of sick bullshit you want to do!" she screamed. "But don't call me at a two thirty in the fuckin' morning, and try to get me involved in it!"

Marty heard the phone slam down. He hung the phone on it's cradle, and as he came into the living room, he shrugged his shoulders and said, "I don't think she was into it."

The next morning when he came home, Cherilyn didn't appear to be upset at all. She just looked at him and said, "What am I going to do with you?" He told her that he was sorry, and she said, "I'll forgive you, Marty. Live and let live...right." But he had broken her heart, and she would never forget it.

For the next few weeks, Marty and Wade concentrated on putting a band together. They found a couple more players, and began to practice regularly. Sam Moyer played banjo and keyboards, Bill Parker became their drummer, and Graham Shurtliff handled the bass. They did a few covers of the San Francisco bands, and a lot of 'Country Rock'. A few of the latter, were originals by Wade and Marty.

In the meantime, Rowena did her best to try to make up with Cherilyn. Little by little, she began to get underneath her skin, in a way that Cherilyn was unwilling to admit. As mad as Rowena could sometimes make her, she felt a strange attraction to her. Rowena sensed it and slowly took advantage. They went out a few nights together, and when the guys practiced, they went clothes shopping at the mall. One afternoon, Rowena tried to show her how to strum a guitar. As she stood behind her, she pressed her breasts against

Cherilyn's back and brushed her lips across her neck. Cherilyn was surprised to feel herself getting aroused, and afterword, while in the bathroom, she realized that her panties had become wet with her sap. She slid her hand between her legs, and put an end to the sweet torture that Rowena had unwittingly set in motion.

About a month later, the whole crew was at 'The Tumbleweed'. Marty and Wade's temporarily unnamed band warmed up the crowd, and then 'The Dishes' came on to perform. The girls ripped it up. They didn't flaunt their sexuality, and the music rocked. Rowena had taught Cherilyn the words to one of their songs, and they invited her up to sing harmony. She had consumed just the right amount of alcohol to give her the necessary courage to pull it off, and she had a blast.

Afterwards, the two couples decided to go ghost hunting. Marty had mentioned that he liked that kind of stuff. Cherilyn wasn't thrilled. She didn't like being scared. Despite her apprehension, she agreed to go along, and they all piled into Wade's old suburban. They breezed by a couple of spots, and then Wade pulled onto a really creepy dirt road. He said jokingly, that it was called 'Weirdo Way'. But it was actually named 'Richmond Hill Lane'. About halfway down the road, there was a wooden sign post that read, 'Richmond Farm Cemetery'.

Wade began to tell the history of the small cemetery. "Back in the 1800's there had been a farm here, and the Richmond family owned this property for decades, 'til the last of 'em died off, 'round the turn of the century. A couple of 'em had met a violent death, and a young boy died at the age of six years, from some disease or the other. The cemetery ain't got nothin' but family members in it, and as the legend goes...a few of 'em don't know they're dead. They say a woman in a white dress, a tall man in a hat...and a little boy haunts this whole damn area...road included."

Marty thought about trying to scare Cherilyn, but he knew she'd be pissed, and would probably want to leave. He tried anyway. "Look over there! I seen him... I seen him!" Cherilyn screamed and dug her fingernails into his shoulder. "Oww, woman! Take it easy on the carcass!"

"Alright!" Wade scolded, "If we don't keep quiet...we ain't gonna see no ghost's, now are we!" He opened his door and got out. "C'mon, don't be scared." The other three followed. Rowena lit up a cigarette and offered Marty one. "You oughta quit them," Cherilyn nagged.

"SSSSHHHH!" Wade eyed everyone like a dad who was about to send his kids to bed. They all stood in silence for about fifteen minutes. Wade whispered, "Did it turn cold around here, or what?" Marty felt something touch his hand, but before he could say anything, the driver's side mirror began to swivel on the truck. Wade started to say, "What da..." Cherilyn and Rowena started to scream and everyone jumped into the truck.

Wade started the Suburban, shifted into drive, spun it around and kicked up gravel all the way down the road. When they hit the pavement, he peeled out and kept the pedal to the floor for at least five miles. On the way, everyone was in an uproar, all yelling at once. "What just happened?" Wade drawled, still shaken with fright.

Rowena laughed, "It was the guy!"

"I seen the woman!" Marty lied.

Wade insisted, "I tell ya... the little boy was right there!"

"He touched me!" Cherilyn shivered.

When they got back to the house, they all laughed and admitted it had been fun. Marty said, "That place was for real."

"I told ya!" Wade laughed.

Suddenly, Marty looked at Wade and said, "That's it...that's the name of our band! We'll call ourselves...Richmond Hill."

All Wade could say was, "Brilliant!"

6

Cherilyn was genuinely straight, but Marty could tell that she was curious and weakening. He had been watching Rowena hitting on her for months. Finally, one night, as Wade and Marty watched a baseball game, Cherilyn and Rowena quietly slipped off to the bedroom. Rowena had talked Cherilyn into taking a quaalude. And she'd had more than enough to drink. The drug and booze cocktail had made her very horny, and with her defenses down, she had succumbed to Rowena's advances.

Some time had passed when Marty excused himself to go to the bathroom. He did his business, and as he came out, he could hear a female moaning softly. Curious, he peeked into the bedroom to see both girls completely nude and Cherilyn's wide open legs, as Rowena joyfully lapped on her pussy. Cherilyn saw Marty and smiled haughtily, and he turned and went back down the hall.

The next day, Cherilyn felt embarrassed about what she'd done. Even worse, she was sad because Marty didn't even seem to care. She blamed her encounter on him, and said that she didn't want to see Wade and Rowena again.

Maybe Marty didn't mind, but Wade did. He'd had it with Rowena. They had been drifting apart for a while, and her little tryst with Cherilyn was the last straw. Not so much because it had hurt him, as much as he knew that it would eventually break up his friends. He told her that they were through and kicked her out of the house. He had hoped that she'd go home to New York, but he was wrong. She went straight over to Marty and Cherilyn's. She told them that Wade had wigged out, and that she needed a place to stay, until she got on her feet. She wasn't sure if she was going to stay, or go back home. Surprisingly, Cherilyn agreed with Marty that they should take Rowena in.

Marty talked to Wade to see how he felt about the arrangement. He told him it was alright. "She was getting too weird for me," he told Marty. "I just wanted her out. I'm through with her, but I didn't want to see her homeless. I should have known that she'd go to your place." They agreed that there would be no hard feelings, and that the two of them would remain friends. They also agreed that the band would stay intact. "One more thing," Wade warned. "Watch your back."

Once in the same house with Cherilyn, Rowena intensified her pursuit. She wanted her bad, and after a while, Cherilyn quit resisting.

Partly because Marty had not yet tried to intervene. The band was starting to pick up steam, and he was always out with Wade. He had no idea that Rowena was in love with Cherilyn, and she thought that he didn't care. The more that the two girls got it on, the more Cherilyn discovered that she liked it. She began to realize that she'd had it in her all along.

7

The girls removed their clothes, then they moved the kitchen table out of the way and placed several quarts of cooking oil near the middle of the floor. Marty loaded film into a movie camera at the counter. They were preparing to make what would be his first pornographic film. Marty had always enjoyed watching women masturbate, and he loved girl on girl sex. It had recently occurred to him that he could film these erotic sequences, himself and keep them for posterity. He had done some research about filmmaking techniques and what type of camera to use.

The whole evening had been planned. It wasn't hard to talk Rowena into it, but as usual, Cherilyn wasn't sure. She really was still a good girl, teetering on the edge of propriety and restraint. Now, Marty was once again asking her to do things that made her uncomfortable. Things that she once believed to be wrong. But she was slowly beginning to succumb to forbidden desires, that had been burning inside of her for months. All Marty wanted, was for them to have a little fun. He didn't realize he was pushing her into the arms of another. Reluctantly, Cherilyn agreed.

The three of them purposely got smashed on a mix of pills and booze—the girls more so than Marty. Certain depressants were known to make women horny, and Rowena and Cherilyn were no exception. With his two willing—albeit anesthetized—subjects in tow, he was almost ready to begin. His naked starlets, on the other hand, were becoming restless and drunker by the minute. They had begun to clown around, and when Marty looked up, Rowena was on her hands and knees, and Cherilyn was riding her like a horse. He laughed, and suggested that they get warmed up with some foreplay of the sexual kind.

Under more private circumstances, the two women would know exactly what to do, but their movements appeared to be awkward at first, undoubtedly and understandably at feeling self conscious of being filmed. Especially Cherilyn, whose blushing face openly betrayed her false sense of bravado. Marty found it endearing that she genuinely appeared to be embarrassed to do something sexual. Yet, at the same time he thought that it actually enhanced the eroticism of the moment—in essence, displaying the carnal transformation a woman experiences, as she passes through the threshold of tentative uncertainty, and into the wanton realm of unbridled lust.

As Marty fiddled with his camera, Cherilyn looked over at him and complained, "C'mon, Marty...are you getting this? Are you filming? Because if you don't start soon, we're going to take this to the bedroom and leave you here to play with yourself."

"That's right," chimed Rowena. "What is up with you and that camera? Use it or lose it, sweetheart."

At that, everyone laughed, and Marty assured them, "Okay, okay...I've got it. Continue, ladies... By all means, continue."

Slowly, things began to heat up, and soon Marty's dick began to swell in his pants at the sight of the two beautiful women kissing. For a moment, he started to forget what he was doing, and he had to resist the urge to fondle himself.

The girls embraced each other closely, breasts brushing, nipples hardening, hips undulating in rhythmic unison, as one delightful sensation after another began to sweep through their bodies and down to their loins. Marty instructed them to change positions, and as they did, he was thrilled to capture the conspicuous wetness that was beginning to appear between Rowena's thighs.

He was glad to see that the girls were getting the hang of it and had seemed to lose their inhibitions, but by now they were no longer acting, and for that matter no longer paying attention to him. He was having a little trouble keeping his artistic composure himself, and when Rowena began to slide a vibrator in and out of Cherilyn's vagina, and then into herself, Marty became so excited, he almost dropped the camera.

"Alright, girls," he interrupted, almost reluctantly, "time for the oil." The women ignored him, and Rowena began to massage Cherilyn's nipple with the vibrator. In mock director's fashion, Marty scolded, "C'mon, ladies... the oil...let's focus, please!"

Both of the girls started to giggle, as they poured the slippery substance over themselves and massaged it into their skin. But as they began to explore the more sensitive areas of their bodies, their frolicking slowly returned to arousal. Soon they were sucking on each others breasts, their tongues gliding over basted boobs. Far from being sated, they headed south, hungrily devouring the glistening oasis that lay between their luscious legs. The slickness of the oil on the linoleum floor made the scene all the more interesting, as the girls wrestled to get a taste of each others vaginal delight. Marty moved in for a few close up shots of the girls' tongues, enjoying their furry feast. He circled around them and moved back again, making sure to get a clear view of all the action.

He had gotten what he wanted on film, now it was time to join in the fun. He turned off the camera and began to undress, and as the girls writhed in blissful unawares, he slid himself in between the two of them. Cherilyn was so horny, that she begged Marty to fuck her in the ass. Of all the things he'd experienced sexually, he had never been with a woman who would let him perform this kind of act. For a second, he actually felt a bit of moral apprehension about it. But only for a second. He grabbed what was left of the oil and doused himself copiously, until it spread over his belly and thighs. He pulled Cherilyn back on top of him, and she slowly descended the length of his shaft.

Rowena began to rub Cherilyn's clit with the vibrator. She started to moan, and as she arched herself back, Rowena pushed it into her vagina.

Soon, Cherilyn felt herself beginning to cum. "Don't stop! Ohh, please Rowena..." Marty began to cum, and his semen exploded into her ass. "Ohh...fuck..." She moaned, and then she slumped forward into Rowena's arms.

Afterward, the girls were enjoying a hot shower together, when Marty climbed in. Cherilyn protested, "Marty, there's not any room!" But when he ignored her , she said, "Okay...I was done anyway," and climbed out.

The details of the perversion laced encounter they had just experienced lingered fresh in Marty's mind. "I did get a rush out of bangin' her that way," he mused. But he also felt like he had sullied her somehow. To him, it seemed like something a man would do to defile a woman. "Why, would she want to get it in the butt like that?" Did Cherilyn feel a need to be punished, or was it only that she found it to be pleasurable. He didn't even know why it bothered him. Indeed, Marty had done—and would still do—some kinkier things than that.

"It's cool," he thought. "I'm up for anything." But he did care, and maybe it was because he loved her. As Rowena washed his back, he said, "I wonder what it felt like?"

"Why don't you ask her," she replied, and she began to stroke his cock. He quickly stiffened in her hand. The thought of Rowena jerking him off in the shower turned him on. She continued to massage his back with the soapy wash cloth, and she worked her way down to his buttocks. Marty was in heaven. The combination of the warm pulsating water and Rowena's sensual touch, was bringing him to orgasm.

She began to lather the crack of his ass, and then she pushed her fingers into him. He started to pull away, but as she deftly worked her fingers inside of him, he began to cum. His semen shot from his body so quickly, that it hit the shower wall a foot away. As Rowena finished her oriental magic show, Marty thought, "Now, that was different."

The next day, Marty did ask Cherilyn how it felt. She told him that it hurt at first, but she was so loaded and turned on that it didn't matter. He had thought that she was able to take him with such relative ease that she might have done it before. He asked her if she had, and she admitted to having done it with Steve plenty of times. The thought of her, fucking Steve, made Marty jealous. He wondered why the thought of her with men bothered him, when he didn't mind her with women. "Maybe, it's because they posed no real threat," he thought. But he had let one small detail slip past him. In the midst of their tryst, he hadn't noticed that it was Rowena's name that Cherilyn had whimpered, as she was about to cum.

8

It was a rare occasion that Marty and Cherilyn found themselves alone, together. Rowena had gone to work, and they decided to go out and have some fun. Just the two of them. It was the perfect opportunity for them to try and rekindle the romance that had once thrived in their relationship.

To Marty, it seemed as though their time in Germany had been like a fairy tale. He knew that since they came back to the states, the everyday grind of reality had caused him to become complacent and take his woman for granted. Cherilyn just wanted things to go back to the way they were, when they fell in love.

As Cherilyn was getting dressed, Marty poured her a glass of wine. He told her that she was looking good. "Even better, with your clothes off," he teased.

"Flattery will get you nowhere," she teased back, "now let me finish." But he had other ideas. He took her in his arms and kissed her. "Please, Marty...not now. I'm almost ready."

Marty persisted. Before she knew it, his hand was between her legs, fondling her crotch. She tried to push him away. "Marty, no!" He pushed her onto the bed, tugging at her clothes.

Giving in, Cherilyn said, "Here, let me do it." She undid her jeans, and he pulled them off of her, throwing them onto the floor. He began to pull her panties down, and then he violently ripped them away from her body. "Hey, those were my favorite," she whimpered, now beginning to feel cheap and humiliated. This wasn't her idea of fun. She laid there, trying not to feel anything, as he sated himself with her unwilling flesh.

Cherilyn wasn't much in the mood to go out anymore. Marty had just helped himself to her, like a before dinner snack. She was tired of his bullshit. He begged her to go and promised that he'd make it up to her. But she'd had enough. "Fuck you, Marty," she cried. "Go out with yourself."

To add insult to injury, Marty took her up on it. "Whatever you say," he sighed. He shook his head and went into the kitchen. Cherilyn could hear him talking to someone on the phone. When he came back into the bedroom, he grabbed his jacket and said, "I'm going over to Wade's. I'll see ya, later." He turned to leave, and she thought about stopping him, but her pride wouldn't let her. She heard the front door close, and by the time she made it out onto the lawn, he was halfway down the street.

She felt a wisp of cool air against her skin and realized that she was naked from the waist down. She went back into the house and sat at the kitchen table. "It's over," she said out loud, and she began to cry, harder than she had, since she was a little girl.

When Rowena came home, she started to climb into bed with Cherilyn, but she asked to be left alone. "Okay, darlin'," she replied, "if that's what you'd like." As she got up to leave, Cherilyn grabbed her arm and begged her to stay. They held each other in silence for a while, and Rowena could feel Cherilyn's tears begin to run down her chest. Cherilyn grazed her fingers up Rowena's thigh, and she opened her legs for her. She kissed the tears from Cherilyn's cheeks, and then they made love, until they heard Marty's van pull into the driveway.

9

Their relationship was falling apart. Marty was always out with the band, and he was barely paying her any attention at all. Except, for when he wanted to use her body as a play toy. He seemed to have lost respect for her, and hadn't told her that he loved her for months. Cherilyn looked at the engagement ring on her finger, and knew in her heart that they would never get married. The month of May was long past. It had given way to June and July. "Summer's almost gone," she thought. "Soon everything will begin to die."

She decided to talk to Marty about her feelings, and one afternoon she came straight out and asked him what he wanted. "Are we still committed to each other? Is it me? Have I done something wrong? What is our problem, Marty? I just don't know what to think, anymore!"

"I'll tell you what our problem is!" he said. "It's that damn

Rowena! She's like a fuckin' disease! We need to get her the hell out of our house!"

To Marty's surprise, Cherilyn took offense and tore into him. "Rowena has done nothing, but treat me good! You're the one that's been taking me for granted and treating me like a whore!"

The next day, on the way home from work, Marty bought a dozen roses. He knew that he had to give it another try. He gave the flowers to Cherilyn, along with a card, expressing how much he still wanted her and cared for her. She couldn't help but notice that the word love was conspicuously missing from the handwritten sentiment. Happy that he was even making an effort, she let it roll off her back, hoping that she would hear it from his lips before the night was over.

They went out to eat, and afterword, they decided to go for a beer. Rowena was working again at 'The Tumbleweed', so Marty suggested that they try somewhere else. Somewhere else turned out to be a dive called 'The Well'. It was a rowdy place that featured country music, and the type of crowd you'd find at a rodeo.

They had a few drinks, but only enough to put a relaxing glow to an evening that they both hoped would have a happy ending. Cherilyn's mood began to lighten up, and after a while, her displeasure with Marty slowly melted away. As they danced, he held her close and kissed her tenderly, not wanting to make the mistakes of a few days before. For most of the night, their eyes never strayed far from each other. At closing time, they decided to go for a drive and find a place where they could leave the world behind. At least for a little while.

They went to a spot at the end of a dirt road, that led to a cliffside. It was a place that teenagers used for drinking parties, and to make out. Luckily, they found it all to themselves.

Marty pulled over and turned off the ignition. He didn't waste time. He put his hand between Cherilyn's legs, and she said, "Wait, I have to pee." She climbed out and started to undo her jeans. Marty got out of his side and walked around to her. He lit up a cigarette and leaned against the van, as she squatted next to it. He watched, as her waterfall began to cascade down between her thighs, and form a stream on the ground beneath her.

When she'd finished, she pulled up her pants and asked, "Do you always have to stare when people are trying to urinate?" He opened his fly and turned to her. "I don't know, sweetheart...how's it look to you?"

As Marty relieved himself, Cherilyn shook her head and walked to an overlook. She gazed out at the city lights in wonder. "It's so beautiful," she murmured. He came up behind her and held her tight. A long sigh escaped her lips, and she could see her breath in the cool evening air. "Oh, Marty...what's happening to us?" she softly cried. A tear began to run down her cheek. "Why, do you always have to be such an asshole?"

They sat on the cliff's edge and threw stones out into the darkness, every now and then hearing one splash in the creek, far below. They made love in the dirt on a moonlit night, as if they were the only two people on the face of the earth. Afterward, they each pointed to a star and named it for one another. When the air began to chill they climbed into the back of the van, and snuggled amongst the blankets and pillows that were kept there for just such an occasion.

Cherilyn fought the urge to tell Marty that she loved him in fear that he wouldn't say it back. Later, in hindsight, she would wish that she had. But on this night she was glad, at least that they would fall asleep in each others arms, for the first time in quite a while.

In the morning, just as dawn was breaking, they awoke to someone knocking on the back door of the van. Covering themselves, Marty opened the door to see a cop, who had come upon them while making his rounds. "Everything alright in here?" he asked, almost embarrassed that he'd interrupted the two lovers. Marty and Cherilyn just looked at each other and said sheepishly, "Everything is fine officer...just fine."

The evening ended better than it had started. But neither one of them had made any real commitment to change the destructive path they were on. It was a temporary fix, and even they knew that some patches don't hold. Real trouble was brewing, and the lid was about to come off.

10

Up to this point Rowena had been trying to placate Marty in order to keep him off balance, and off her back. But now, she had decided, was the time to make her move and take Cherilyn away from him. She knew that their relationship had been running on auto pilot. But most important of all, she knew that Cherilyn was far more into her, than Marty. She began to openly shower her with gifts and romantic evenings. Finally, she came right out and told Cherilyn that she loved her. To hear someone say those words after so many months made Cherilyn's head spin. She wanted to say it back to her, but this was still new and strange territory for her, and she was scared. She wanted Rowena, but she was afraid to leave the kind of life she was so familiar with.

Marty, for his part, had finally begun to realize what was going on. He had found the scented panties, jewelry and other sensual gifts that were laying around their bedroom. The fragrance of Rowena's perfume on his pillow was enough to make him realize that things had gotten out of hand. When he confronted Cherilyn about it, she told him that he was letting his imagination get the best of him.

One evening, as Marty and Cherilyn laid in bed watching television, they began to make love. Suddenly, Rowena came into the room and climbed into bed with them, with a big bowl of popcorn. Cherilyn pushed Marty off of her. He desperately tried to get back in between her legs, but she sat up and said, "I can't do this." Marty became enraged and yelled at Rowena to get out of their room. Cherilyn said, "Leave her alone, Marty."

"What's wrong, Marty? You used to go for this sorta thing," Rowena said cuttingly.

Marty couldn't believe that it was even happening. It was like a nightmare. He just wanted to wake up. But the fact of the matter was that this was his wake up call. He told Rowena to get out of his house, and stay out. Cherilyn started to protest, but he told her to shut up. "Unless, you want to go with her!"

He grabbed Rowena by the arm and led her to her room. He told her to start packing. Cherilyn came into the room and told Rowena not to leave. Marty tried to push her out into the hallway, and during the struggle, she scratched his face. Fueled with adrenaline, he smacked her across the mouth with the back of his hand. Her lip immediately began to bleed. Rowena jumped onto his back, but he flipped her onto the floor.

Cherilyn ran back into the room and picked up a hair brush from the vanity. As he came towards her, she swung, hitting him hard upside the head. Dazed, and on instinct, Marty hit Cherilyn with a right cross, sending her into the wall. She started to cover her face, and then slumped to the floor, unconscious.

Marty had never fought women before, and his reaction time was slow. When he turned around, Rowena charged him and kicked him square in the groin. She was horrified to see that it didn't seem to phase him. He was fired up. He grabbed Rowena by the throat and lifted her into the air. He slammed her against the wall, directly above Cherilyn, and let her drop on top of her. As she lay in a heap with her lesbian lover, Marty pointed a finger at her, and told her to disappear.

Marty had slept late into the afternoon. He was sore all over, and when he looked in the mirror, he could see the claw marks on his face. When he went into the kitchen, he saw a woman sitting at the table with Cherilyn. For a second, his heart skipped a beat. Until, he realized that she was only selling cosmetics. But Marty could see in her eyes that she was suspicious. Cherilyn had a black eye, and her lip was swollen. He had scratches on his face. It wasn't hard to put it together. He poured a cup of coffee and went into the living room. He lit up a cigarette, and as he blew the smoke into the air, he began to realize that it was over. He thought hard, about all they'd been through together. He thought about the night before, and the pitiful look on Cherilyn's face, just then in the kitchen. "How did this happen?" he thought.

After the woman left, Cherilyn came into the living room and held Marty tight. She tried to comfort him, and tell him that it would be alright. He told her that he loved her, but he'd made up his mind. She could either stay there with Rowena, or he'd take her home to her mother. Either way, the two of them were through. Cherilyn didn't try to argue. She decided to go home.

PART FOUR

1

Cherilyn and Betty had already gone into the house. But Cindy stood on the sidewalk, and as Marty climbed into the van he could hear her voice behind him. "I told ya, he was no good." He shifted into drive and steered down the quiet neighborhood street. Looking in the side view mirror, he saw that Cindy was gone. At the end of the street, he sat at the stop sign. He thought about going back. "Turn around, and go tell her that you love her." Just then a horn honked behind him, and he pulled out onto the road.

As he drove, Marty remembered saying goodbye and thanks to Uncle Josh. He recalled his apology to Wade for cutting out on him, and the whole fiasco with Rowena. He began to think about Cherilyn again, and his emotions welled up inside of him. He thought about the ride back to Palo Alto. They had taken almost the same route as the one they'd taken on the way down to Albuquerque. Only this time around, they had stopped at the Grand Canyon, and decided to spend a couple of days there. When they arrived, they rented a room and got settled in. After freshening up, they went to the lodge and signed up for a guided tour. The tour guide told them that they were fortunate to get in, because most travelers make reservations in advance. He advised them of what they would need to bring with them. It was an overnighter, and it was lucky for them, that they did have sleeping bags and other camping equipment in the van. Most everything else was provided as part of the tour.

By then they were starving, so next it was off to the dining room for an excellent dinner. Afterward, they went for a walk, and by the time they got back to their room, they were so tired from their drive, they both fell fast asleep. In the morning, they had breakfast, and then they met up with their tour group. They set off on horseback, down a trail which led them to the bottom of the canyon. They were taken aback by the sheer beauty of the terrain, and more so by it's vastness. There before them, flowed the Colorado River and the smaller tributaries that emptied into it. Streams wound their way under natural bridges, and led to hidden lagoons at the bottom of breathtaking waterfalls. Gulches and rock formations that had taken millions of years to develop, seemed endless.

Marty was astounded to think that it would take almost a lifetime to explore the entire canyon and wondered if there could even be places yet to be discovered, that may never have been trod upon by a single human being. He hoped at that very moment, that there were still places like that in the world, and for the sake of the earth and mankind, that it would stay that way. They made camp at the end of the day, and after a good meal, everyone sat around the fire and told their stories. Most of them talked about where they were from and where they had been. The guides told tales of the Native Americans, who once called the land they were sitting on home, and the white men, whose explorations sometimes took them into the canyon, but never back out of it.

After a singalong or two, and a few required ghost stories, the group slowly turned in for the night. Once he was sure that everyone had fallen asleep, Marty tried to get Cherilyn to fool around, but for the first time since he'd known her, she felt uncomfortable about doing it in a compromising situation. "What if somebody wakes up?" she worried.

"Let's take a little walk, then," he prodded.

"No, Marty," she sleepily insisted, "I'm so tired." She turned her back to him and told him to go to sleep.

In the morning the group had breakfast and several much appreciated cups of coffee. Then they began the long trek back up to the top of the canyon. When they finally got back to the lodge, Marty and Cherilyn finished the day souvenir shopping, and had another good meal, before returning to their hotel room for a warm shower and a welcome bed.

As they laid there, they tried to talk things over and attempted to heal their wounds. Be it the fun they had on the tour, or just the magic of the canyon itself, something brought their feelings for each other to the surface, and it slowly led to the inevitable. They began to kiss, tenderly at first, but soon they were all over each other, and their clothes came off fast. As Marty's hand wandered down to her crotch, Cherilyn suddenly felt like she had to pee. She excused herself and went to the bathroom. She was in there for a while, and when she returned, Marty could see that she had been crying. She slipped back into her panties and pulled them up. His heart sank. "Was she having second thoughts?" When she climbed back into bed, and he kissed her, his face became wet with her tears. He was about to ask her what was wrong, but she cut him short. "I got my period," she cried.

Marty took it as a sign. "There's no turning back," he thought. Cherilyn had fallen asleep in his arms, but he laid there awake, thinking about everything. Back to the time he had advised her to loosen up and live a little. The fact was, that she had done a lot of living. She was a vibrant fun loving woman, who had given him some of the best times he'd ever had, but it wasn't enough for him.

The sun was setting in the evening sky, and Marty pointed the van in the direction of the only place he could go. There really was no turning back, especially for Cherilyn's sake. He had almost succeeded in destroying her. Thank goodness she had gotten away from him, before he could do even more damage.

2

It was late when Liz pulled up to her house to find Marty sitting alone on her front lawn. They went inside, and he told her everything. Someone else in Liz's shoes would have been delighted with this turn of events, but she truly felt sorry for him, and even more so for Cherilyn. After he had gotten everything off his chest, they decided to call it a night. Marty slept on the couch. Liz told him to sleep well, and she'd see him in the morning, but he tossed and turned. He suddenly felt lost, as though part of him had died.

The next day, while Liz was at work, Marty pondered his options and decided to take some classes. He'd had to work a few night shifts in the mill and rail yard, and he wanted to get away from that. He was tired of dirty jobs. A career in advertising was what he wanted. He'd use the a government loan to help to finance his schooling. He went over to the community college to sign up for the start of the next class.   That evening, when he told Liz the news, she was thrilled. After dinner they went out for a walk and stopped for ice cream. Liz made sure to order something different from Marty, so they could share their cones.

When it was time for bed, he got ready to settle down on the couch and told her to sleep tight. "Oh, for heaven's sake, Marty," she told him, "come to bed." He snuggled up to her that night, but he didn't attempt to go any further than that.

Marty spent the next day looking for a job. He answered an ad for part time shipping and receiving at a lumber yard. He was offered the position on the spot, and he accepted. The money would help pay the rent, and get him through school.

That evening they went out for Chinese food and stopped at a bar for a few beers. When they got home, they smoked a joint and watched television. Liz laid across the couch with her head in his lap. Marty was already beginning to get ideas. He couldn't be this close to a hot girl like her, and be expected not to make a move. At bedtime, he just couldn't resist.

As they laid there, he began to inch his hand from her belly to her breast. He felt her nipple harden at his touch, but he chickened out and moved his hand away. She grabbed it and put it back where it was. As Marty fondled her, she began to sigh, and she pressed her bum against his crotch. He slid his hand into her panties, and discovered that nature had already begun it's warm, wet anticipation of their impending lovemaking.

As he grazed his fingers over her furry mound, she reached her hand between them and began to stroke his cock. He pushed his fingers inside of her, and she panted, "Marty...just fuck me!" They both removed their underwear, and he slid his arrow between her thighs. She grabbed ahold of him and guided him in. Liz rubbed her clit, as he slid in and out of her, and she begged him to go faster. His belly smacked against her soft buttocks, and he felt his climax burning inside of him. He told her that he was about to cum, and she said, "Go ahead, baby...so am I!"

3

If ever there was a soulmate for Marty, Liz was it. He had an uncontrollable attraction to her. When it came to pure sex appeal, she turned him on more than any other woman. Her shoulder length blond hair and pink nipples were just part of the reason he couldn't resist her. At five foot four, and not quite one hundred and twenty pounds, she had a gorgeous body. Her exquisite legs, led up to a perfect heart shaped ass, and except for at the office, she almost never wore a bra.

But it wasn't just her looks. She had an endearing quality about herself. She understood Marty and knew how to put him at ease. She could see inside of him, and he felt the same way about her. She was smarter than he was, and he felt safe with her. Even when she was bad, it was hard to see her that way. And most of all, she was willing to take just about anything Marty had to dish out.

Like any new lovers, Marty and Liz did everything together.

They went to rock concerts in San Francisco and hit all the good restaurants. Liz still loved sports, and the two of them went to as many games as they could. They loved to hang out in the coffee houses and listen to music, and the prose of the beat poets.

One weekend, they went hiking in the foot hills of Marin County. The spent the day climbing, and at the top of one mountain, they could see the whole city and the ocean beyond. They camped out and made love by the fire. Marty told Liz that he was in love with her. She smiled and hugged him tight. "It's about time," she said, "I've only loved you, since forever!"

4

Liz was in the backyard hanging laundry out to dry. She was wearing a bikini and trying to get some sun, while she did her chores. Marty sat at the picnic table drinking a beer and watching her. Liz looked great. To him, the view was spectacular. He lit up a cigarette, and he complimented her on a job well done—among a few other things. She came over and sat on his lap. "What other things?" she cooed.

He put his hand on her thigh, and then he pulled it away, shaking it in the air as if he'd been burned. "Oooh, that's hot!" he teased.

She giggled and said, "You're bad."

He asked her, "Is this a beautiful day, or what?"

"Oh, it is a beauty."

"Not nearly as beautiful as you, though," he told her. "Not even close."

"Well now...you must want somethin', cause it's pilin' up out here."

"How do you like that," he protested.

They both started to laugh and Marty kissed her. Liz's tongue darted into his mouth, and she could feel him beginning to stiffen up, beneath her. She slid her hands down between her thighs and began to fondle his crotch. "Let's go inside," she begged.

"No..." he said, "let's do it right here."

"You gotta be kidding, Marty. Someone might see us."

"So, what if they do," he replied. "That's the fun of it."

She stood up, and Marty opened the fly of his pants. Her face turned red, as she pulled her bikini aside. She climbed on top of him, and a sigh escaped her lips, as she slid down the length of his shaft. She wrapped her arms around his shoulders and held close to him, afraid to look around.

Marty teased her. "Go on, baby...no one's lookin'. Except, for that perv' in the window over there."

"Ohh, don't..." she giggled.

"You know ya want it," he dared. "Your pussy is so hot."

She started to wriggle her bum in his lap, and then slowly began to glide up and down.

Within minutes, she'd forgotten all about her nervousness, and she started to feel horny as hell. Liz couldn't believe she was getting laid, outside, in broad daylight. Now, the idea that they were possibly being watched by someone made her feel wild. She began to lick Marty's neck, and she bit his ear.

"Mmmm...it feels good," she growled, a guttural tone in her voice. She grazed her lips against the side of his face, and he could feel the cadence of her breath, keeping time with their lovemaking.

Liz was becoming more turned on by the second, and watching her, was making Marty lose control. She felt herself just on the verge, and she told him to let her have it.

He picked her up and carried her to the edge of the table. She leaned back, and he began to slam his length in and out of her. He started to cum, and moments later, Liz's own orgasm shuddered through her loins.

When they were finished, Liz fell back on the table. Marty pulled out of her and went inside. She laid there for a half an hour, before she got up and finished hanging the clothes.

5

The two lovebirds decided to go back to Pittsburgh for
Christmas. It had been a while for Marty, yet he wasn't very anxious
to see everyone. Aunt Nina was depressed, still grieving over the loss
of her husband. "Christmas just isn't the same without your dad," she
told Liz. For Marty, it just wasn't home anymore. To him, it was a
dark place, and one he'd just as soon forget. They also had to spend
the entire time at arms length. In California, no one knew who they
were. At home, they had to lay low, and keep their secret hidden.
They stayed with Liz's mom and occupied separate bedrooms.

At home, their circle of friends was different, too. Most nights,
they went their separate ways. Marty bumped into Nelson at a bar, one
evening. Beth had been long out of the picture, and he and Nelson
made up. "Hey, ya can't blame the guy," Nelson said. "If a woman
offers the fruit...the man is gonna take it. I knew she was a whore

when I met her." Beth wasn't a whore, but Marty understood where Nelson was coming from.

He told Nelson that he should come out west. "It'll be like old times... only it's way better out there. And the weather is beautiful." Nelson assured him that he would keep it in mind. Marty figured that he would never show. He was just glad that they were still friends.

One night, Marty was feeling low, and he needed someone to talk to. Liz had gone out, and he was home alone with Aunt Nina. Coming home hadn't been good for him. Aside from patching things up with Nelson, it was a waste of his time. And he hated that he and Liz couldn't be together. Aunt Nina had gone to bed, and he decided to go over to Liz's sister Virginia's house to cry on her shoulder.

Virginia's husband Bill was working the late shift at the mill, and the kids were in bed when Marty got there. She had already been drinking for a while, and she was glad to see him. She got Marty a beer and offered him a chair at the kitchen table. He chugged his beer and Virginia got him another one. He laid out some lines of cocaine, and they drank and talked for hours. Virginia challenged Marty to admit it. She knew that he and Liz were together. She had watched the two of them since the days that they were kids. She knew that they couldn't be near each other without having sex.

Marty told her that they were living together, and that they were in love. He said that he wanted to spend the rest of his life with her. But he knew, sooner or later, he'd wind up hurting her. He told Virginia that he almost couldn't turn down any woman if she gave him the chance. They decided to move their conversation to the living room couch, and Marty splashed a few more lines on the coffee table. The wheels in Virginia's head began to turn. She'd always been jealous of Liz and Marty, and she wanted him now. It couldn't delight her much more, than to be the one to turn a good thing sour. She was really drunk and very horny. She figured the best way to console Marty was to let him get into her pants.

She began to kiss him, and he pushed his tongue into her mouth. His hand moved to her breast, and she pulled her shirt over her head. They stood, and as she tugged at Marty's shirt, he began to undo her jeans. He slipped his hand inside. As he grazed his fingers over her bush, he felt the end of a tampon. "It's the end of my period," she assured him. "I had it in, just in case."

Virginia started to remove her jeans, but she stopped and led Marty back to the bedroom. "Don't start without me," she teased and excused herself to the bathroom. When she returned, he was kneeling on the bed, warming himself up for her. "Hey...no fair," she giggled. She quickly peeled off the rest of her clothes and joined him.

She wrapped her arms around the back of his head and pushed her tongue into his mouth. He slid his hand between her thighs and forced his fingers inside of her. Her legs weakened, and she pulled him down on the bed. She opened her legs, beckoning him to devour her, and Marty immediately helped himself to her delicious offering.

Virginia heard herself moan, as his tongue penetrated her opening, and it suddenly dawned on her, that her kids might hear them.

It didn't matter. The attention he was giving her, was about to make her cum. She let him bring her just a little further, and then she pulled him up to her. He began to suckle her breasts, and she reached down and stuffed his cock into her vagina. He began to glide in and out of her, and she held onto his buttocks, pulling him to her with every stroke.

The bedroom door was open, and Virginia heard the toilet flush. She told Marty to get up and close the door. "I don't want my kids to see me gettin' fucked," she slurred. But he just kept on screwing her, and she was too horny and stoned to do anything about it.

Marty got home before Liz, and didn't bother to clean himself up before he went to bed. When she got home, she came into his room. She was loaded, too, and wanted some attention. She started to suck Marty's cock, and as he began to get hard, he wondered if she could smell Virginia's scent on him. Whether she did or not, he never knew. As Liz slid herself down onto him, she drunkenly cooed, "Do me like you love me, Fucker!"

6

On the plane heading back, Marty was very disappointed in himself. He'd let his sexual hunger cloud his judgement again. He had never felt so bad after any of the other wrong things he'd done. Liz noticed that he seemed down, and had hardly said a word. "You're awfully quiet," she said. "Are you alright?" He told her that he was, and that she needn't worry. "Typical," he thought. "Here I am doin' her dirty...and all she cares about, is that I'm okay."

But it was the same old Marty. Liz gave him a smile, and he began to loosen up. And the devious side of him began to reappear. As he thought about his tryst with Virginia, and then about Liz sucking him afterward, he got a little turned on. Especially, at the thought that Liz had unknowingly gotten a taste of her sister's pussy.

A few weeks later, Marty had forgotten all about it. Things had been going great for the carefree lovers. One afternoon, they drove into the city and spent a few hours at Golden Gate Park. It was a gorgeous day. The sunshine in California was magnificent. It shone warm on their faces, and glistened on the ripples in the bay. The days of Hippies and Be-ins were pretty much over, but the vibe was still unmistakably there. Some kids were flying kites, and they let Marty and Liz give it a whirl. Liz got the kite up in the wind, and began to run with it, Marty and the kids giving chase. There was a hotdog vendor in the park, and they treated the kids for letting them join in their fun.

A few hippies remained. They saw young mothers nursing their babies, and sat in on an impromptu sing along with a group of local musicians. Marty had his trusty harmonica with him, and he played along to a couple of folk and blues numbers. Liz couldn't remember a better day in her life. Marty couldn't help but to think about how lucky he was to be with Liz, in one of the most beautiful cities in the world. It was exactly what he'd always dreamed of.

They started to go out socially more often, and they began to develop a circle of friends. Roxanne Lesh worked with Liz, and had been to the house a few times, since Marty had moved in. She was probably Liz's closest friend, and she was a no nonsense kind of woman. Through her, they had met Randy and Gwen Sanchez. They had a place in Alameda, and had held several great parties there. Roger Grant was a co-worker of Marty's. He was an easy going black man with a wonderful sense of humor. His girlfriend was Luann Belich, a sexy little blonde, who had eyes for Marty.

As well as house parties, the gang liked to tear it up in the hills of Marin County. Randy and Roger both had four wheel drive trucks, and everyone would jump in the back, usually with a quarter keg of beer. They'd build a nice fire, and music was provided by their truck stereo's. Someone always had pot, and occasionally, they'd do some 'LSD'. Usually, one couple or the other, would wander off for a quick screw in the darkened woods.

Marty and Liz were head over heels in love. There was no way that two people could be any closer. One night in bed, Liz jokingly remarked, "We should just get married. What the heck...we already have the same last name."

"Yeah, you're right, baby," he replied. He kissed her and rolled over on his side, facing away from her. "Let me sleep on it...will ya."

But the conversation—joking or not—must have been a bad omen. It made Marty think about things, and little by little, he began to change. Things started to go wrong between the two of them, and they made a bad decision that would eventually tear their loving bond apart. They started using drugs like quaaludes and heroin. This was nothing new to Marty. He had used both of these drugs before, but he did them sparingly. For some reason, this time around, the two of them hit it full tilt. At parties, they would consume several different drugs on top of gallons of booze. Sometimes, they'd share a whiskey bottle, laced with pills. They began to shoot heroin, and as the months passed, their consumption of the drug increased to catastrophic proportions.

135

The two of them were doing so much dope, they were becoming junkies. One morning, Marty woke up feeling like he had a bad case of the flu. He told Liz, and she said to hold tight. She came back and gave him a fix of heroin, and he began to feel better. "I didn't know smack was a cure for the flu," he said.

"It's not," she replied. "You're an addict."

7

It was as if the Devil himself, had come calling in his favor for letting Marty and Liz have their illicit affair. Once a loving couple, they had turned mean, especially to each other. What was most puzzling, was that Liz had never been that way her whole life. It seemed that Marty had done a good job of rubbing off on her. They were a mess, and needless to say, it got worse.

Marty started to sell dope to get money, and keep them supplied. At parties, they hardly ever used to leave each other's side. But now—more often than not—they'd go their separate ways. While he would peddle his drugs, she would go prowling for her own kinds of fun.

Liz began to stop at the bar after work. At first, it was one night a week, then it was two and three. She started coming home later and drunker, as time went on. But it wasn't just the booze that was keeping her out at night. She had called home one evening to tell Marty that she was at a place called 'The Oasis'. He knew for sure that the bar was always noisy. Yet, it had seemed awful quiet on her end of the line. He could swear though, that he heard what sounded like a shower, running in the background.

Marty had thought that it was so ironic how things had been turned upside down. Now, it was the woman coming home late from work, and the man saying, "But honey...dinner's getting cold!" What goes around, comes around.

There were times, when Marty would leave Liz stranded at parties, while he looked for dope. Sometimes, he wasn't there to stop her from succumbing to the attentions of others. More often, it was someone else, who gladly attended to the needs of Liz's open legs, when he wasn't around. It didn't help matters much, when out of the blue, Nelson showed up in town with his friend Pete Young. Marty was elated to see him. The new arrivals found an apartment in San Francisco, and he began to spend a lot of time carousing with them. Nelson always had some scheme going, and it usually involved dope. Liz saw this as a major problem.

One night, Marty and Liz went out to a bar called 'The Cactus Lounge'. The evening started out just fine. They played pool, and an excellent sounding rock band began to perform. Their conversation was casual at first. But as the night wore on, Liz began to get loaded. She had taken the usual mix of pills, and chugging her drinks wasn't helping any. She started to bring up their problems, but Marty didn't

138

want to talk about it. "What's the big deal?" he snapped. "Don't be such a pain in the ass!"

"I'm tired of you acting like you could take it or leave it!" she cried. "You make me feel cheap! You make a fool of me in front of everyone! I've got nothing to hang on to! I need you to act like you want me! I need you to make me feel like you love me!"

Things went downhill from there. She began to hang all over everyone in the bar—men and women. Marty suddenly felt a tinge of jealousy, and he began to pound beers himself. Soon, the both of them were pretty well oiled. The band took a break, and someone went up to the microphone and announced that it was time for the evening's main event. It turned out that it was a wet t-shirt contest. All of the participants were asked to come up to the stage, and strip to their shirts and panties. Liz decided to participate, and as she and several other girls danced onstage, they were doused with water. The guys and a few women took turns putting money into their panties. Then things started to get wild.

Liz noticed Marty between one of the girls' legs, money clenched in his teeth, attempting to tuck it into the crotch of her panties. This immediately sent her temperature level through the roof. A guy came up to her and inserted a twenty dollar bill into her panties. Liz thanked him by pulling him to her, and pushing her tongue into his mouth. When she looked again, the girl had pulled her panties aside for Marty, while he hungrily lapped away on her glistening mound.

Despite her feelings of jealousy, she began to become aroused.

By now, the people in the bar saw what Marty was doing. Liz went over and pushed him aside, and began to lick the girl herself. She slipped her hand into her own panties and feverishly rubbed her clitoris. Marty used the opportunity to slip outside with another woman. By the time that the owner, the bartender and a boyfriend intervened, Liz had started to cum. Luckily, 'The Cactus Lounge' was a pretty rough place, and they had seen it all before. All they did, was throw Liz and a few others out of the place, and no charges were filed. Still, public lewdness was frowned upon in most respectable drinking establishments, and Marty and Liz were banned for life.

Liz found Marty and the woman on the side of the building, engaged in a lip-lock against the wall, his cock wrapped firmly in her hand. She walked over to them and pulled the woman by the hair, and as she turned, Liz punched her in the mouth. "Get lost, bitch!" she warned. The woman wiped the blood from her lip and staggered back into the bar. The action had left Marty breathless and aroused, and he figured that she was going to take a swing at him next. Instead, she knelt down in front of him and finished sucking him off. When she was through, she stood up and slurred, "Keep it in the family...you fucking asshole!"

Liz insisted on driving home, and Marty was too loaded to disagree. On the way, she could hardly keep the car on the road. She sped through a stoplight, and when Marty told her to slow down, she pushed the pedal to the floor.

On the front porch, he put his hand on her crotch, and she

pushed it away. "Don't touch me...you fucking pig!" She started to hit him, and she dropped her keys. She pushed him aside and ran around to the back of the house. Marty gave chase, and when he caught her, they fell to the ground. He slapped her, and she struggled to get out from under him. As they fought, he tried to kiss her, and she spit in his face. He ripped her blouse open, and exposed her braless boobs. He tried to bite her nipples, but she kept hitting him.

He smacked her hard in the mouth and undid her jeans, pulling them down to her ankles. Liz tried to keep her legs closed, but it was no use. Marty slid his hand into her panties and ripped them off of her. He pushed her legs open, and began to lick her pussy, and when he pushed his tongue inside of her, she began to succumb to his advances.

She grabbed Marty by the hair and pulled him up to her. She shoved her tongue into his mouth, and frantically began to tug at his belt. He grabbed her hands and held them to the ground by her head. "Come on, fucker!" she screamed breathlessly, "give it to me!"

Marty unbuttoned his pants and pushed them to his knees. Then he slammed himself inside of her. Liz moaned, as he thrust himself in and out of her. She pulled him to her again, pressing her lips hard against his. She ran her hands across his back, and as the waves of her orgasm spread through her body, she raked her nails into his flesh. Their lovemaking ended as intensely as their fight began. The lines had been blurred between heaven and hell. And pleasure and pain seemed to consume their very beings.

Sadly, they were drifting apart. They didn't even realize what was happening to them. Drugs and outside temptations were killing the passion they once had for each other. Still, deep down inside, they loved and cared for one another. It was still each other that they came home to, most of the time. Marty was a comfort zone that Liz couldn't break away from, yet.

That slowly began to change, as an affair Liz was having started to become more serious. Bits and pieces of rumors started getting back to Marty. And it didn't slip past him, that while she usually came home smelling like antiseptic, sometimes he could detect the smell of aftershave. For several months, Liz had been sleeping with a guy named Mark Grayson. He made everything feel new and fun again. He had been pressuring her to dump Marty. But a friend of theirs told Marty, and without Liz ever knowing, he found Mark and threatened him. Liz couldn't understand why—without explanation—Mark broke it off with her.

8

The party was in full swing at Roxanne's when Marty and Liz decided to sneak off to a bedroom. They had taken some quaaludes, and washed them down with a couple of bottles of vodka. Liz was feeling frisky, and she needed Marty to fulfill her desire. They stripped completely naked, without concern that they were in someone else's house. Liz was hot to trot, but Marty felt the need to tease her. As he knelt between her legs, he told her to make herself cum. "Oh, Marty, please! Just put your cock in me!" she begged.

He insisted that she do as he'd told her, and she reluctantly began to rub herself. At first, her movements seemed stiff, but in minutes she began to loosen up. She closed her eyes and spread her legs wider. Her body started to undulate, and he marveled, as a river began to flow from her opening. This turned him on, and he began to stroke himself. "Uuuhh..." she sighed, "mmmm..."

Liz pushed her fingers in and out, and over her clitoris. Marty was about to go over the edge when she began to cum. He waited until the waves of her orgasm had almost subsided, and he pushed himself into her. As he glided in and out of her, she could feel herself beginning to cum, again. Marty could feel his own orgasm aching to be released. She watched his face, as his semen exploded inside of her. She closed her eyes and let herself go.

Even though her hunger had been sated, Liz was miffed at Marty for teasing her. When they came out of the room, they began to shove each other, playfully at first. But then it got ugly. Liz punched Marty in the mouth and tried to kick him in the groin. Roxanne came around the corner, just in time to see Marty shove Liz across the kitchen, and into the garbage bin. She laid there for a second, sprawled over the trash on the floor. Liz looked over at Roxanne, and Marty looked at Liz, and they both started to laugh. Roxanne looked at them disgustedly, and said, "You two have got a problem."

She was right of course. They had been on one cocaine binge after another, and then shooting smack to come down. They routinely mixed drugs, and were swilling in a sea of alcohol. They had a big problem, and Marty tried to do something about it.

He asked Liz to quit doing drugs. He said that he needed to stop, and that they should do it together. "We've got a good thing going, baby," he pleaded, "but if we keep on going the way we are...it's gonna come apart." She agreed that things weren't right, but she said it was his fault, and that she wasn't done having fun yet. "You call this fun!" he said.

"Maybe without you!" she said cuttingly. And then she went out without him.

Marty quit doing drugs and cut down on his drinking. Over the course of several weeks, he began to wean himself off of the heroin. He started to play his guitar again, and hooked up with a few musicians. They played together on jam nights at a place called 'The Blue Cafe'. Little by little, he began to feel better. But Liz wasn't responding. She continued to do things to purposely spite him.

A few months later, the tables got turned on Liz. She and Marty had been out bar hopping with the gang. When the bars closed for the night, Roxanne invited everyone to her house to continue the party. Liz said she was tired and begged off, but Marty was game. He kissed Liz and told her to drive safe. She took off, and Marty got in the front seat with Roxanne. Roger and Luann sat in the back. Randy and Gwen followed in their truck. Once at Roxanne's, they built a fire and sat around listening to music. Marty had been watching Luann since the evening began, and by now he wanted her bad. Soon the party began to wind down, and Roxanne said she was going to bed. She told everyone they could crash there for the night.

One by one, the tired guests picked their spot, and after awhile they fell asleep. Everyone except Marty. He finished off the last of a bottle of bourbon, and was feeling horny. He looked at Luann lying next to Roger, and went over and woke her up. They tiptoed around, behind the couch, away from the view of the others. Marty unbuttoned her blouse, and she removed her bra. He began to suckle her breasts, as he rubbed the crotch of her jeans. They both took their pants off, and he pushed her legs apart, to lick her pussy. He pushed his fingers inside of her and pressed his tongue against her clit. "Oooh...if you keep that up, you're gonna make me cum," she quivered. She pulled him up to her and pushed her tongue into his mouth. "Mmmm...I love the taste of my pussy." Marty teased her with the head of his cock. "Stick that peener in me, or else!" she ordered.

Marty took aim, and she led him into her heavenly oasis. He pushed in and out of her, slowly at first. As he started to go faster, Luann felt him begin to swell inside of her. "Don't you cum, Marty!" she scolded. Pushing on his chest she said, "Me on top," and they switched places.

She began to glide up and down the length of his shaft, and within minutes, she was about to cum. She slid up and down one more time and panted, "Now, Marty!" She could feel his cock swell even bigger, as his juices shot up his shaft and exploded into her. She arched her body back and gasped, and then she threw herself forward, hands on Marty's chest, and pressed her clit against him. She fell on top of him, and laid there for a while. Marty couldn't help but be impressed with her expert nurturing skills. She rolled off of him, and they fell asleep in each others arms.

He awoke first in the morning. He woke Luann, and she got dressed, slipping back over to Roger, before anyone else saw them. At least, they thought that no one had seen them. Later that day, as Marty and Liz were on their way to the mall, she suddenly blurted, "I hate Luann!" But she never said anything else about it again.

9

Marty was loading a customer's truck at work one day, and when he turned around, Cherilyn was standing there. He asked her how she was, and she told him that she was doing fine. He said "What the heck are you doing, way out here?" She explained that she had a cousin that worked there at the lumber yard, and he'd get her stuff at his employee discount. "So, do you have your own place?" she asked.

"Naw, I'm staying with Liz." He didn't tell her the rest.

Cherilyn reached into her purse and pulled out her engagement ring. She took Marty's hand and gave it to him. "I've been hoping that I'd get a chance to get it back to you."

"Aw, it's yours...I don't want it back."

"Keep it," she insisted. "If you meet someone else someday..."

Marty surprised Liz, and gave her the ring for her birthday. He thought that it would make her feel better, and bring some luster back into their relationship. Liz loved the ring, but it was too late. Her love couldn't be bought, and neither could her dwindling libido.

Liz had gone to the store one day, and when she came back, Nelson and Pete were there talking to Marty. She had a feeling they were up to no good. She got her answer, when Marty told her that he was going to Mexico with Nelson, to get some pot. Liz blew up.

"You're outta your fucking mind! Do you really think you can get across the border with dope?"

"Nelson has a foolproof plan..."

Liz cut him off. "Go ahead, Marty! Go with Nelson! My mother's not feeling well, and I'm going to see her! I'll probably stay awhile! If you go, I probably won't be here when you get back!"

Marty left with Nelson and Pete that evening. They drove through the night, and Marty thought of Liz the whole time. They stopped in Bakersfield to get a bite to eat. He tried calling her, but there was no answer. They continued on, and by the morning they had reached Santa Ana. After breakfast, as they were heading to the car, Marty said, "Guys, I'm going back."

"What did you say?" Nelson asked in disbelief. "You're planning to abort! But why... oh, why... my intrepid partner in crime?"

"I gotta get back, before Liz takes off."

"Alas...a man's got to do, what a man's got to do."

Nelson drove Marty to the bus station, and they wished each other good luck. Marty waved, as they drove away. He bought a ticket for the next bus back to Berkeley. But by the time he got back home, Liz was gone. The engagement ring was on the kitchen table.

He sat down and smoked a cigarette. He knew it was over, anyway. He'd finished school a couple of months before, and he really had nothing to hold him there. He packed his belongings and loaded them into the van. Before he left, he wrote Liz a note. It read, 'I love you, Liz. You're the only one for me'.

PART FIVE

1

There was always something about leaving town, for Marty. He was feeling the come and go blues again, and this time he was headed for Fresno. He'd gotten an early start, and he couldn't have picked a better day of the month to do it. It was Friday, the thirteenth. Marty wasn't the suspicious type. If anything, he'd always had good luck on that particular date. Still, he did take some things to heart. When it came to his relationships, he knew that something's were just meant to be.

When he got into town, he checked into a motel, then he grabbed something to eat. It wasn't hard to find a watering hole. And for the next few evenings, he spent his time in 'The Lamp Post'. It became his command center, where he drank and mapped out his plans. He looked in the want ads, and quickly found an apartment. Within three weeks time, he'd found a job. He got in on the ground floor of an ad agency, and he was in business. Not knowing anyone at first, made it easy for him to stay away from drugs, but Marty was Marty. He had his good side, that wanted to do the right things. Then, there was his bad side, that just wanted to tear it all apart. It wouldn't take long for 'Bad Marty' to get into mischief.

And so went life at the ad agency. Marty really had his pick of women in that place. Marty's boss was a female, who had a soft spot for men. A horny, hot soft spot, that got wet, and made her squirm in her seat, when a guy sat next to her. She liked to call Marty into her office to discuss his job performance, with the door closed. He loved to slip his hand up under her skirt, and feel how wet her panties were, while they discussed business. Tina Barton was married, and she was having an affair with another female co-worker. But she wanted Marty bad, and he knew just how to make her feel good, on top of the desk, in the chair, in the closet.

Her car was in the shop once, and she called Marty to give her a ride to work. The car windows were still fogged up when they pulled into the parking lot. Marty liked Tina, and thought she was sexy and hot, in a country girl kind of way. She had a good heart, and could be very thoughtful. But to most of the other women in the office, she could be catty and vengeful, and sometimes she would look for reasons.

She definitely didn't like Selena, who had recently been directing her intentions toward Marty. Selena loved to do things to get his attention. Like the time he walked by her desk, on his way to the copy machine. As Marty sauntered by, he noticed that Selena had her skirt hiked up in her chair, and she had her fingers in the crotch of her panties. She smiled at him, as her hand moved up and down, and he could clearly see that her fingers were inside of her.

Marty could feel himself becoming aroused, and in seconds he was fully erect. Selena suddenly gasped, and appeared to be having an orgasm. He almost came in his pants, and was so turned on, he had to go into the mens room and relieve the pressure.

Selena Bettencourt was from Raleigh, North Carolina. Her father died from emphysema when she was nine years old. Her mother remarried when she was fifteen. The guy was a millionaire. Her mother cut her off soon after, for being a wild child. Selena was exotically beautiful. She had light brown hair that hung to her shoulders, and the sleek body of a movie starlet. With her pouty lips and sleepy eyes, she had an air of sexual promiscuity about her that was hard to resist.

A few weeks later, Marty had to work late, and he noticed that Selena did, too. Most of the other employees had left for the evening. When she saw him taking some files into Tina's office, she followed. Closing the door behind her, she looked around the room and said, "Tina's got it good in here...don't she." She ran her fingers across the top of the desk and teased, "Why don't ya show me what Tina does at her desk, Marty. What does she do in here with you?"

Marty knew what was about to happen, and his cock began to stiffen. Selena hiked up her skirt, and lowered her panties down her thighs, stopping at her knees. She climbed onto the desk and cooed, "Be nice, and help me with those." Marty obliged, and slid them off. She pulled her sweater up over her breasts, and began to play with her nipples. Marty unzipped his pants, letting them drop to his ankles. She pulled him close, and pushed her tongue into his mouth. Selena's kiss aroused him more than any other woman he'd known. He kissed her neck and suckled her breasts. His dick never felt so hard.

She grabbed his cock and stuffed it into her opening. As Marty thrust himself in and out of her, she began to buck herself against him. Soon, she was about to cum, and she sucked hard, on Marty's neck. "Mmmm," she moaned. Suddenly, his semen shot out of him, and to Selena, it felt like a cannon had gone off inside of her. She teased him. "Whoa, darlin'...has it been that long?" Marty started to pull back from her, but she held him tight. "Not so fast," she scolded. "I want to feel you shrink inside of me." He pulled out of her anyway, and she pouted. He watched, as his semen dripped out of her, and onto Tina's desk. Selena looked down, and knew what Marty was thinking. "Let's just leave Tina a nice little gift of appreciation, for letting us use her desk," she said, with an evil tone.

She slid her ass across the desk, and began to straighten her skirt. Marty picked up her panties and handed them to her. She handed them back and said slyly, "You keep them, darlin'. Maybe you can get some use out of them." As they left, he thought for sure that Tina was going to know. But she never found out, and she thought the stain on her desk was coffee.

As they spent more time together, Marty began to learn that Selena's eagerness to tantalize was almost like an art form. One evening—unbeknownst to him—she stuffed her vagina full of chocolate covered cherries. Wearing nothing but white cotton panties, she began to perform a belly dance in front of him. As the candy melted, it started to run out of her, and he thought that she was having her period. When she slid her hand into her panties, and then put her fingers in her mouth, he at once became sickened and aroused. It was only after she invited him to taste her sticky concoction, that he realized what it was. Selena became the perfect subject for Marty's films. She was so horny, that she would sometimes get lost in her own ecstasy, and forget that the camera was there. Other times she would ham it up, giving kisses to the lens, before continuing to pleasure herself.

There were other things about Selena that Marty would soon find out. He began to realize that his beautiful girlfriend had a dark side. She was a sadomasochist, who was into hitting and bondage. She liked to cut herself, and others, and got off on sucking their blood. She told him, "When I cut myself, it doesn't hurt. It feels good...like all the pain inside of me, flows out with the blood."

Selena also liked heroin, and she was already a junkie. This was bad for Marty, because he'd been trying to ease off of the stuff. Keeping up with her, meant that he would return to some bad habits, and more.

Whatever misgivings he might have had about Selena's personal preferences, he was able to overlook them. He had his own obsessive perversions, and most of them had to do with sex. As long as she was willing to get it on anytime, anywhere, anyhow, he was content.

As time went on, the unbridled passion between them started to evolve into something more. It was no longer just for kicks. They were beginning to fall for each other.

For Valentine's day, they decided to go out for dinner and a movie, and Marty made sure there was time for a romantic prelude, to the evening ahead. Things started out in the usual manner when he presented Selena with the required candy and flowers. Then he gave her a sensual massage, which inevitably led to some steamy lovemaking.

He worked her over from head to toe, and as his hands deftly moved over her smooth skin, Selena felt like she was in heaven. Eventually, he found his way between her legs, and gently began to graze his fingers over her already dewy pearl. She raised herself up to her hands and knees to make things easier for him. "I need it bad, baby," she teased. "I want my pussy stuffed full of your cock." Marty was already way beyond aroused, and he gladly tended to her need.

Selena was so turned on, that within minutes she was about to cum. Marty sensed her urgency, and he gave her the full length of his cock, with every stroke. She quivered in ecstasy and bucked herself hard against him.

Suddenly, he pulled out and asked her to roll over. "Marty!" she cried. "I was cumming!" But she did as he asked, and he pushed right back into her. Selena's belly began to flutter, and soon she was almost back to where she left off. Marty watched himself glide in and out of her swollen nether lips. The sight tweaked his senses, and he felt his cock jerk. His semen shot into her with such force, that it squirted right back out of her. That feeling, was all it took to send Selena over the edge. She clutched her pillow and moaned, as her climax shuddered through her ravished loins.

Marty wasn't finished. He rolled off of her, and left her there on the bed. He returned with a basket filled with her favorite perfume, the latest record albums and some sexy underwear. He drew her a candle lit bath with rose petals and serenaded her on his guitar, while she bathed. "My pussy's still tingling," she whimpered, as he dabbed a soap bubble from the tip of her nose.

Selena dressed herself in a particularly fetching manner—wearing a miniskirt and a tight sweater over braless breasts—which effectively had Marty's tongue, and his dick wagging. Now it was time for the fun to really begin.

After dinner, as they sat in a darkened movie theater, the wheels began to turn in Selena's dirty little mind. Just as the magic of the evening would have it, the theater was almost empty, except for a man sitting alone and a few other couples. There was plenty of space between them for intimacy.

She took Marty's hand and slid it up her thigh, and under her skirt. He took the hint, and began to caress her crotch. He could feel her panties begin to dampen, and she squirmed in her seat at his touch. Marty was becoming a bit turned on himself, and Selena returned the favor. She unzipped his pants, and began to stroke his already rock hard penis.

"Just a second," she sighed and hastily removed her panties. She climbed onto Marty's lap and guided him into her dusky jewel. Her tongue darted into his mouth, and soon they were both beginning to cum. Suddenly, Selena let out a lusty moan that echoed through the darkness—thoroughly enjoying her climax, and not caring if everyone in the theater knew it.

Marty suggested they make a quick exit in case there was a chance that they might be discovered. With the movie only half over, they slipped out of the side door, leaving Selena's panties on the seat behind them. On an occasion when most couples find ways to express their love for each other, this horny duo could find a way to make even cupid himself blush.

Tina was jealous of the two of them, and she needed to find a way to get rid of Selena. As fate would have it, Selena played right into her hands. Customer's checks that came into the office were kept under close scrutiny. But even so, several had come up missing. Tina discovered that Selena had stolen them to get money for smack. She pinned it on her, and had her fired.

Marty couldn't fathom how Tina could hate Selena so much. Then, a close friend of Tina's filled him in. Tina had an affair with Selena, and fell in love with her. But Selena's needs were too much for Tina to satisfy, alone. One night, Tina had gone out to visit a friend. When she arrived back home, she saw Selena driving away. She asked her husband what Selena was doing there, and he told her that she had been looking for her. Tina was ready to let it go, until she found Selena's hair brush on her vanity.

Later, when she asked her about it, she explained that she'd left it there from a night that she'd been there with her. Tina didn't believe her. After that she never trusted her. Selena grew bored with Tina's insecurities, and their relationship came to an end. Tina told Marty to stay away from Selena. It was too late. He was in love with her, and Tina got screwed again.

Marty found a place to keep his creative juices flowing. When he'd first arrived into town, he spent a few evenings in a pub called 'The Lamp Post'. He took Selena there, and it became their place to hang out. They made some friends there, and Marty met a guy named Bruce Philips. He was a musician and songwriter, who had been playing the local circuit. He told Marty that he hadn't been able to click with anyone up to that point, and they started to jam together.

Bruce agreed to play the bass, and he brought in a drummer named Hugh Samuels. After a few weeks of rehearsing, Marty bought a 'Gibson Les Paul' electric guitar and a 'Fender Twin Reverb' amplifier from a guy named Keith Wilson. Keith had originally planned to join up with them, but instead, was about to spend time in prison for selling marijuana. They got Selena to share lead vocals with Bruce, and a band named 'Sweet Jane' was formed, in Keith's honor. Doing original material, they developed a heavier sound, more akin to the british bands.

The only problem was that drugs flowed plentiful through the doors of the clubs they played in. Sometimes Selena would get so out of it on heroin, that they had to play without her. Marty got a funny feeling that was hard to ignore. He shook it off anyway, hoping that history wouldn't repeat itself.

Luckily, Selena found another job at a record store called 'The Listening Post'. They decided to move in together, and they found a cottage at the end of a secluded country lane. A creek ran through the yard, and a small bridge led up to the driveway. Selena didn't mind playing house with Marty. He was different, and even though he loved her, sometimes he would act as though he could care less about her. This intrigued her, and more than she wanted to admit, he had her wrapped around his finger.

For a while, they lived the happy life of getting things for their house and continuing their sexual escapades. One night Bruce called, and Marty made plans to meet him. Selena pouted. She didn't want him to go. She was having a bubble bath, when Marty came in and said, "I'll see ya, later."

"What...no kiss?"

He leaned in to oblige her request, and she wrapped her arms around his head and shoulder. Suddenly, she pulled him into the tub with her. Marty felt angry at first, but as he looked into her hypnotic eyes he began to melt. The combination of her wanton sexiness, and the feeling of being clothed and wet in the tub started to arouse him. He pressed his lips hard against hers, and they began to writhe breathlessly in the splashing water.

Marty opened his fly, and she guided him into her yearning cootchie. He thrust himself in and out of her, and was so turned on, he quickly reached the verge of orgasm. "No!" he gasped. "I want this to last!" He pulled out of her and took his clothes off. He slid back into the tub, and this time they made love slow and easy. Afterward, they went to their bedroom to continue the fun. Before they fell asleep, Selena told him that she loved him. Needless to say, Marty never met his friend that night.

Sadly, things weren't going to stay happy for the two of them. Selena's heroin addiction was beginning to take it's toll on her. It was ravaging her body and eating away at her mind. And she would become violent if she really needed a fix. Marty had started to use again, himself. It didn't take him long to slide back into the routine of a full blown junkie.

His libido began to come and go, and sometimes he would neglect Selena for days. "I can't even get laid around here!" she'd say in disgust. "I need fucked, damn it!" Marty didn't seem to care. He'd tell her, "Go fuck yourself." And she'd do just that. Some nights, he'd lay in bed, and listen to her moaning next to him, feverishly pushing her fingers in and out of herself. She had no idea how much he despised himself for not wanting to make love to her. She began to resent him, and would hold sex back from him, in return.

When Selena failed to show up for another rehearsal, Bruce gave Marty an ultimatum. "Either she goes, or you're out, too," he demanded. "We already have someone to replace her...so...what do ya say?"

Marty had no choice. "Yeah...I agree," he told him. "She probably won't care, anyway."

Bruce introduced him to the new lead singer. Her name was Brigid Duncan, and after listening to her, Marty was impressed. The girl could really sing. But she came as a package deal. Her sister Lisa played organ and piano, and they brought along a bunch of songs they had written. The two of them turned out to be the missing pieces the band had needed.

When Marty told Selena, it didn't seem to bother her at all. The band had just been a source of fun for her. But when a record producer came to one of their gigs, and expressed interest in helping them get a recording contract, Marty started to spend more time with them, than he did with her. Slowly, a little jealousy began to creep in. Especially, when she noticed the way he was looking at Brigid during one of their shows. She started to think that maybe he had a reason to side with the others, and it began to eat her up inside.

Finally, she broke down and confided her feelings to him. She told him that she was sorry that she was a junkie and was messing everything up. "Brigid is so pretty," she cried. "I know that you want her."

Marty was truly touched that she had opened herself up to him like that. He told her that she needn't worry. "There's nothing between me and her," he promised. He told her that he loved her, and at that moment, he meant it.

Over the next few months, he kept his drug use in check, for Selena's sake, and his own. He began to pay more attention to her, both in and out of bed. Selena promised to slow her drug use down, too, and for a while it appeared to be working. But it was particularly hard for her. Something had to replace the heroin, and for her, it was blood.

3

Marty showed up a few minutes early to pick Selena up at 'The Listening Post'. He got out of the van and lit up a cigarette. She had wrecked her car, and her constant problems were driving him crazy. She was having a harder time quitting the dope, and she was always cutting herself. She was a mess, and didn't look, or act like the beautiful woman that he once knew.

Her co-workers started to leave, and she was the last one to come out. She locked the door and said, "Let's get the fuck outta here...I need a drink!" They got in the van, and she started to bitch about her tough day. Marty snapped. He grabbed her arm and said, "Look at this! Between the needle marks, and the cutting, you can't even see your skin anymore! You look like a freak!"

She jerked her arm away and lit up a joint. "Ya want some?" she asked.

He didn't answer. He pulled out of the parking lot and started for home. Selena took a long drag and blew the smoke into Marty's face. "Let's stop somewhere," she begged. "I need to get really drunk, okay." He kept driving out of town, and suddenly, she dropped the joint onto her lap.

As she searched around for it, Marty could see down her blouse. She could feel him staring at her, and when she looked up, she began to tease him. "So, darlin', do ya like what ya see?"

"Yeah, I guess I do," he replied, his face turning red. "They looked so good, I just had to take a peek."

"You guess. Is that all?"

"Well...you know what I mean."

Selena giggled. "I'll let ya feel me up, for a couple of vodka's on the rocks." He had to give her points for persistence and creativity. Besides, when she put it that way, he couldn't turn her down. He turned the van around and drove back to 'The Lamp Post'.

Marty got something to eat, and tried to make sure Selena didn't get too loaded. It was no use. By the time he'd gone up on stage and jammed with a few of the guys, she had vomited into her purse, as she sat at the bar. Later, he found her sleeping on the pool table. He thought it best to leave her there, until he was ready to go.

On the way home, Selena began to squirm in her seat, and when he looked over at her, she was fondling herself. She pulled her panties aside and cooed, "This is still good...ain't it?" He shook his head in amazement. A few minutes earlier, he had been thinking about

165

having to help her to bed. But Selena was far from through. Marty could see that her pussy was beginning to moisten, and when she penetrated herself, the crotch of his pants began to spring to life. She opened her blouse and brushed her fingers across her nipples. Marty almost wrecked the van.

He pulled off the road and onto their lane. In front of the house, Selena jumped out and ran inside. When he caught up with her, she was in the kitchen, waiting for him. She stripped down to her panties, and began to finger herself. Marty looked like a dog without a bone—only his was getting harder by the second.

He went over to her and pushed his tongue into her mouth. She reached down and opened his fly, pulling him by the cock, and rubbing it against herself. He slowly worked it inside of her, and she quivered from the sensation. He picked her up and carried her over to the table. As he pushed in and out of her, Selena draped her arms around his shoulders and began to suck on his neck, softly at first, then harder.

She started to buck against him, and then she bit into his neck. Marty was about to cum, and even though it hurt, he couldn't stop. Selena began to lick his neck, and he felt something drip down to his shoulder.

He pulled away from her and saw his blood on her lips. He became so turned on, that he came as he stood there. Selena knelt in front of him to finish sucking him off. As her lips moved up and down his shaft, he yanked her up by the hair and gave her a backhand across the mouth. Selena looked at him in shock, and then she clawed his face. Marty punched her again in the mouth. She fell against the sink, and put her hand to her lips. She'd bitten her tongue, and her lips began to swell. He went over and hit her again, harder this time. She dropped to her knees, barely hanging on to consciousness. Blood was pouring from her mouth.

He helped her to her feet, and then he slammed her, face first into the refrigerator. Selena slouched over onto the table and moaned. "Whore!" he yelled. "Do you like to bleed?" He pulled his pocket knife out and opened it. He wildly began to slice her back, and he could see blood appear from her wounds. He threw the knife on the floor, and began to pull Selena's panties down, ripping them from her at her thighs. Through all his rage, Marty still had an erection, and he got behind her and forced his cock up into her ass. As he thrust himself in and out, her knees began to buckle. He held her up against the sink and continued to slam into her.

Suddenly, Selena seemed to come back to life. She propped herself up, hands on the top of the counter and panted, "C'mon, Marty, fuck my pussy!" Marty pulled out of her ass and pushed hard into her vagina. "Don't stop...you bastard! Fuck me, you son of a bitch!" With each stroke, she began to moan, "Aaah, aaah...mmmm, aaah...oooh, you're gonna make me cum!" His anger melted from him, and he felt bad for Selena. "Okay, Marty...Cum, now!" she cried.

When he'd finished, she turned to him and smiled. Marty couldn't believe that she was still standing. He knew that she had purposely goaded him into the beating he had just given her, and that she'd enjoyed it. He just didn't understand why. She just winked at him and wrapped her arms around him, as if she never wanted to let him go.

4

One morning in late spring, Marty noticed a pretty new secretary at the agency. He started to flirt with her and found out that her name was Novalee. She was from Los Angeles. Her parents still lived there. Her mother was a school teacher, and her father, an air traffic controller. When she was sixteen, Novalee ran away to be a hippie, but when she found out that she would be shared by every guy in the commune, she decided that a change in scenery was in order. She had been living in Fresno with her Aunt Brenda, who upon her arrival insisted that she finish high school and get her diploma.

Marty told her that she had just about the prettiest name he had ever heard. She was a nineteen year old brunette, but she looked like she was fifteen. Her bright blue eyes and beach babe demeanor had struck his fancy. She was just what the doctor ordered, and he went after her. Novalee thought everything about Marty was great. After a few weeks, she began to fall in love with him.

"She's jailbait," Tina teased. "And, what about Selena? What about me for that matter. I think it's been a while since we discussed your work habits. Come into my office," she ordered. Marty unzipped his pants and sat in Tina's chair. She knelt in front of him, and began to suck him hard.

"I think, I wanna leave Selena," he confided.

Tina hiked up her skirt and pulled her panties aside. "Well, it's about time you dumped that slut," she replied, as she climbed onto the chair and slid down his shaft. "Haahh!" she sighed. "That feels just about right."

5

Marty couldn't let Novalee find out about Selena. It was his plan to get rid of her, and have Novalee move in with him. To his good fortune, Novalee wasn't very pushy. One afternoon, he asked her to go for a walk in the woods with him. She gladly accepted his invitation. He just wanted to spend some time alone with her. Novalee had the same idea. As they walked down the path, she let Marty hold her hand. It was a beautiful day, and after awhile, they stopped to watch the riffles in the creek. He asked her, "If there was anything you could have right now...what would it be?" Novalee had a pretty good idea what she wanted right then.

"I'll show you mine, if you show me yours..." she cooed. She pulled him to her, and slid his hand into her shorts. She was ready. Marty realized, that not only was she a very beautiful girl, but she was also a very horny one, as well. He pushed his fingers inside of her, and she sighed, "Mmmm, that feels better."

She let Marty play with her for a while. Then, she led him to a tree by the path and undid his pants. She bent over and grabbed ahold of her ankles. "Come and get it," she teased. As he stepped towards her, she turned around and pushed her tongue into his mouth.

She pulled her shorts aside and guided him into her. He began to glide in and out of her, slowly at first. Just as their lovemaking was beginning to become more intense, she pushed him away. Marty's patience was wearing thin. She dropped her shorts and wriggled out of her panties, kicking them aside. This time he picked her up, and she wrapped her arms and legs around him. She reached down between her thighs and helped him back into her furry slit. With her back against the tree, Marty was able to slam his length in and out of her. Novalee clung to him, and tried to meet his thrusts half way. She felt his cock begin to swell inside of her, and she knew what was about to come, from inside of him.

Suddenly, Novalee saw someone coming down the path. The woman stopped and hid behind a tree when she saw them. It was Selena. Novalee was about to push Marty away, but she was beginning to cum, herself, and couldn't stop. As her orgasm rushed through her body, she noticed that the woman was looking directly at her.

She watched Selena's hands brush down her belly and between her legs, and she heard herself moan. Selena opened her jeans and slid her hand down into them. When she closed her eyes, Novalee just knew that her fingers were inside of her. She pressed herself against Marty with all her might, and felt his juices shoot deep inside of her. She held him as tight as she could, until the heights of her climax began to subside.

As she climbed down from him, she could feel his semen drip down her leg. Selena smiled mischievously and licked her fingers. She came over to them and knelt in front of Novalee. She licked his semen from her thigh and said, "Naughty, Marty...where are your manners. Aren't ya gonna introduce me to your new girlfriend?"

6

The fact that Marty had cheated on her, did bother Selena. Even though, she knew that she had never really been the faithful type herself. She just didn't see a need to make a big deal out of it. They had long since, quit loving each other, and were basically still together out of a common sickness. She wasn't even mad at Novalee. As a matter of fact, she'd already gotten wet more than once, while thinking about her.

Novalee forgave Marty for not telling her about Selena. He talked her into moving into the house, and they agreed to let Selena stay. It was a bad idea all around. Selena had taken a liking to Novalee, and it was only a matter of time, before she would lay her disease laden hands on her. One evening after Marty had left for a gig, she saw her chance.

Novalee had taken a walk on the grounds around the cottage.

She was feeling a little horny, and behind the cover of some brush, she opened her jeans, and slid her hand down inside. As she pushed her fingers into her cootch, she was startled by a noise. She looked up to see Selena coming towards her. She started to zip her jeans back up, but Selena said, "Please...don't go."

She lifted Novalee's shirt, and began to suck her nipples. The sensation immediately swept through her body, and down between her legs. Selena knelt down in front of her, and pulled her jeans down to her ankles. She began to lick her through her panties, and when she tried to pull them aside, Novalee pushed her away. She said, "Don't do that," and tried to reach down and pull up her pants.

Selena grabbed her hands, and held them behind her legs. She looked up at Novalee, and then she pulled her panties down. Novalee told her, "Please...don't," but didn't try to stop her. Selena pressed her tongue against Novalee's vagina, and began to suck on her clitoris. She began to moan. She put her hands on Selena's shoulders, and she stepped out of her pants. Selena stood, and took her own pants off. They began to kiss and their tongues swirled in each other's mouths. Selena pulled her to the ground. Novalee spread her legs, this time inviting her.

Selena began to lick her pussy and she pushed her fingers inside of her. Novalee felt strange, and yet, she was excited by what was happening. Selena knew that she was nervous, and she thought it was funny. Still, she tried to soothe her apprehension—if only to quench her own greedy desires. "Relax, sweetie...it ain't gonna hurt."

She continued to lap away on Novalee's slowly moistening muff. Selena's tongue was melting her, but the thought of achieving an orgasm in another woman's mouth made Novalee squirm. She closed her eyes, and tried to imagine that it was Marty between her thighs, tenderly soothing her aching wound. Soon, her hips began to undulate, as her fears dissolved into arousal. Selena could see in her face that she was suddenly becoming wrought with desire. She leaned up and pushed her tongue into her mouth. Novalee could taste herself on Selena's lips, and it brought back that funny feeling. But not for long.

They switched positions, so that they were both between each others legs. Novalee slipped her fingers into Selena's slit, and found her hot spot. By now, she was extremely turned on, and instinct had begun to take over. She pressed her tongue against Selena's clit, and spread her open with her fingers. A river flowed from her, as Novalee's tongue glided over her opening, and then inside of her. Selena took up where she'd left off before, and soon both women started to cum—their gratification echoing in the warm evening air. When they were finished, they continued to lay there in that position, spent and pleasurably exhausted.

For the next few days, Novalee mulled her encounter with Selena, over and over in her mind. Never, had she even thought about being with another member of the female gender. Of course, she had never received that kind of attention from a woman before. Now, she couldn't get the memory of Selena's tongue lashing out of her mind— or her loins. She thought that she was in love with Marty, but she was beginning to become attracted to Selena. She couldn't understand what these feelings meant. She only knew that it felt good.

7

Selena was really going down. She had gotten herself fired from 'The Listening Post' for stealing money from the cash register. Her heroin habit was out of this world, and she was cutting herself to ribbons. She seldom left the house anymore, because she was too tired and her arms were too marked up.

Poor Novalee had let Selena take her under her wing. Selena responded by getting her hooked on heroin. The three of them spent most of their time sitting around and shooting up. Marty began to ignore Novalee in the sack, much like he had done to Selena. More often than not, it was Selena's bed that she crawled into at night.

Marty was tired of paying for Selena's dope habit. She hadn't found another job, and she started to become like a vampire, draining him of his money, dope and blood. Several times, she had come to him in his sleep, and either sliced him, or bit him on the neck, each time sucking the blood from him. Sometimes, he'd shove her away, and other times, he'd just let her do it. If he happened to be in the mood, the sensation would arouse him, and then she would climb atop his swollen mast and bring them both to orgasm.

Novalee still cared for Marty, and she had hoped that he felt the same way about her. But as the weeks passed by, his behavior began to make her think otherwise. It had become apparent, that she only existed when he needed her for something, and lately, his treatment of her began to change from indifference to meanness. It wouldn't be long, before he would begin to abuse and torture her into fulfilling a plethora of deviant sexual fantasies.

One afternoon, Novalee went to Marty, and begged him to give her some of his stash. He told her that he was low, too. "What are you gonna do for me?" he teased.

"Please, just give it to me. I'll do whatever you want."

"Oh, really," he replied mischievously. "Then come with me."

She could only wonder what he was up to, as he grabbed his camera and led her down to the basement. They went into the laundry room, and he handed her some clothes. He told her to change into them. "What gives, Marty?" she asked.

"Just do it," he pleaded.

Puzzled, she did as he asked, and removed her shorts and halter top. She dressed herself in the pleated mini skirt and white blouse he'd given her, which made her look like a naughty school girl. "Pretend that you're doing the wash," he ordered.

Novalee pulled some towels from the dryer, and started to fold them. Marty turned on his camera, and began to focus in on her. He knelt on one knee, and started to film. After a minute, he instructed her, "Now...I want you to turn to me, and pee yourself."

Novalee was astounded. She knew Marty was kinky, but he hadn't yet included her in this kind of perversion. "What did you say?"

"I would like you to wet yourself," he replied.

She protested. "Marty...no!"

Marty acted as though he didn't hear her. He told her to pull her hair away from her face. She did as he said. "You, are so hot, baby!" he gushed.

But that didn't make her feel any better. Novalee was hot, and young. Any man would want her, but she had gotten herself in a bad situation. Right then, she wished she had never met Marty. But she needed a fix badly, and she gave him what he wanted. It felt strange at first, actually trying to soil herself. Her mind wouldn't let her do it. She felt a few drops come out, and had the urge to stop herself. "I can't, Marty," she said, and started to cry. She heard him tell her to smile, but that didn't stop the tears from running down her face.

Novalee felt her withdrawal start to worsen, and knew that she had to do it. A few more drops came, and then she let herself go. Her face turned red, as the crotch of her panties became saturated from her leaking spring. It quickly began to spread, and started running down her thighs. She looked down and saw the puddle that was forming at her feet. She felt humiliated. She couldn't believe that a man she cared about would make her do this. She was beginning to realize that Marty didn't really care about her at all.

On the other hand, Marty was very turned on. He put down his camera and knelt in front of her. He pulled her skirt down to her ankles and pressed his face into her crotch. She let him continue for a while, and then she pushed him away. She kicked her skirt aside and removed her panties. She went over to him and pressed her vagina into his face. For a second, Marty couldn't breathe. She let up on him and ordered him to stand up. She knelt in front of him and unzipped his jeans.

Novalee took the head of his cock in her mouth, and slowly ran her tongue around it. She began to slide her lips down his shaft, until she had consumed his length. She bobbed up and down on him a few times, and he began to lose control. As his semen filled her mouth, she thought about spitting it at him. But she took every bit of it and made sure to lick the last drop, as it slowly ran out of him. Finishing, she looked up at him and begged, "Will you get me high, now?"

8

Novalee had descended completely into Marty's world. A slave to heroin, she had fallen head first into a maelstrom of depravity. She had lost her will, and no longer had the strength to say no. It wasn't even as if she had given up and joined the other two. They had kept her in her place, a living doll, with whom they played with at their leisure.

She felt betrayed, but it never occurred to her that she could just leave. Instead, she continued her affair with Selena, for the sole purpose of humiliating Marty. And it worked. Some nights, he would hear the sound of their lovemaking, and he would masturbate.

Marty had been doing a lot of thinking, himself, lately. He felt like he was losing control, and that soon, he would go over the deep end. He was beginning to believe that through all of the debauchery, he had somehow opened a door for a demon to come inside. He had always had a seedy side to him, but now he had become a dope pusher, a whore master and a sadist. He was running a zoo, and he was the zoo keeper. Selena and Novalee had turned into animals, and he, himself had become a predator.

He wondered how his life had turned so ugly. Drugs had a lot to do with it. But it was mostly the fact that he was never satisfied. He never knew when he had it good. He got bored so easily, that even when things were running smooth, he had to find a way to upset the apple cart. Marty thought about his past love's. Back to his mediterranean interlude with Marisa. His affair with Claudia. Much happier times, he thought, much simpler. He thought about how he blew his relationships with Cherilyn and Liz. "Liz," he thought, "maybe there's still a chance."

Just as Marty was beginning to realize that maybe it was time for a change, he received a phone call that made a tough decision that much easier. It turned out that Jenson Talbot, the producer, who had since become their manager, had been a very busy man. "He booked us to play at a festival in Atlanta next month, and then we're going to Los Angeles to make a record," Bruce explained.

"You mean a whole album?" Marty asked.

"Yes...a whole album...probably eight or nine songs."

"Holy shit...that's great!"

"Yeah," Bruce replied, "but there's just one thing," his voice suddenly taking a somber tone.

"What...what is it?"

"Marty...I hate to tell you this...but...you're out of the band."

"What...why..."

"It's just...well...you've just become unreliable. Marty...Marty, are ya there?"

Marty couldn't talk. He was stunned. But he knew it was true. He'd missed a few rehearsals, and then the last gig. "I've become just like Selena," he thought. He heard Bruce's voice and snapped back to reality.

"Marty, are ya still there?"

"Yeah, I'm here," he answered.

"Look, Marty...I gotta go...I'm sorry. Try and get yourself straightened out. I'll be talkin' to ya...okay..."

"Yeah, Bruce...hey...good luck. I'll see ya."

"See ya, Marty."

The train had been rolling out of control for way too long. Marty knew it, but this latest turn of events had left him reeling. He found out through mutual friends that Bruce had hired a bass player and had taken over the guitar himself. The initial shock had worn off, and he was pissed that he wasn't given a warning. But deep down, he realized that it was meant to be. "Oh well," he thought. "Now, I've got nothin' left to hold me here."

That evening, he called Liz. She was glad to hear his voice. He told her that he was in Fresno, and that he was in bad shape. He asked her how she was doing. "Oh, I'm okay," she said. "A short while after you left, I spent a month in a rehabilitation center. I've been clean since then."

"Good for you," Marty said. "That's what I need to do."

"Marty...my mom died. She had a heart attack."

"Damn...I'm sorry, Liz. I..."

"It's just us, Marty. We only got each other, now." Liz started to cry. "Please, Marty...come back. I'm considering taking a job in El Paso. I'll wait for you, alright...but don't take too long."

"That sounds great, Liz. I'm gonna do it. I'm really gonna try..."

"I miss you, Marty. I've been keeping your side of the bed warm."

"I'm already there, Liz. It's great to hear your voice."

"I love you, Marty."

"Me too, Liz...bye."

Marty had meant what he had said to Liz, but it was easier said, than done. He should have just packed his things and left, but he felt bad for the girls. Selena was on cloud fifteen, living in the bizarro world of her dope addled mind. She began to dissipate to the point where she almost never bathed. Most of the time, she wouldn't get out of bed. Finally, Novalee went back to Marty, which left Selena mortally offended. It was a mistake that Novalee would live to regret.

A few weeks went by, and disaster struck again. Novalee got caught fixing dope in her car, at work. She was fired for doing drugs on company property. Luckily, her boss liked her, and saw no reason to involve the police. Tina warned Marty to get away from them. She said, "Those two whores are gonna take you down, Marty. Get outta there, while you still can."

Marty sank into a depression, and started doing more dope than ever. He started to get crazy, too, and Novalee was scared. It had been more than a year, since she'd first met him, and she still didn't know who he really was. Even with all they'd been through, she had remained with him. She believed that they still had a chance together, if only she could get him away from Selena.

She managed to get him out of the house one afternoon, and once alone, she decided to make one last attempt at getting him to see things her way. She convinced him to go to the place where they'd first made love, with the intention of seducing him back to his senses. As they walked along the path, they came upon a swimming hole, partially surrounded by a cliffside and waterfall. They decided to take advantage of their pleasing discovery, and all that mattered next, was who would be the first one in.

The cool water provided a much needed reprieve from the midday sun, but could do nothing to quell the desire burning deep within them. It didn't take long for Novalee to accomplish the first part of her plan. Marty splashed her, and she dunked him in playful retaliation. When he came up for air, he pulled her close and kissed her. The sensation aroused her more than she could ever remember. He pressed his hardening shaft against her and pushed it inside.

A warm summer breeze and the beauty of the landscape, had put them in the mood, and it seemed that serendipity had swung in

Novalee's favor. But afterword, as they began to straighten their clothes, Marty confided that he was going to leave. The revelation hit her like a ton of bricks. "What did you say?" she asked, almost dumbfounded.

"I'm leaving Fresno," he repeated.

"You've got to take me with you," she begged. "Please...take me with you!"

"No," he replied, "I'm going back to where I've always belonged."

Novalee felt like she'd just been punched in the stomach. She began to cry and continued to beg him. "Please, Marty...please! Don't do this!"

He told her that he was sorry for the way he'd treated her, and that he was a better person for having known her. But he was determined to start a new life, and that she should do the same.

Once they were back at the house, she laid in bed crying, until Marty pushed the needle into her arm. When she awoke, later that evening, the memory of his words rang clear in her mind. "A better person for knowing me," she snickered, under her breath. "Hmmff!" She realized that there was no way to change his mind, and she resolved to do as he said. She made a plan to leave in the morning, and she began to pack her things.

9

Still sleepy, she got up and went into the kitchen and made some coffee. She poured herself a cup and fixed a bowl of cereal. She brought her breakfast into the living room and plopped onto the couch. She was enjoying her cereal, when Selena staggered in and sat down next to her. She lit up a cigarette and took a long drag.

Novalee began to feel uneasy, and she got up and sat in the chair. Selena turned the television on and stared at it for a while. "I'd like some breakfast, too," she mumbled. She got up, and went down the hallway toward the bedrooms. Novalee watched cartoons for awhile, and about twenty minutes later, Selena returned with a bottle of vodka.

She sat down on the coffee table in front of Novalee and offered her the bottle. Novalee declined. She could see that under her t-shirt, Selena wasn't wearing any panties. "What are ya lookin' at?"

Selena slurred. "Ya want some of that? You oughta like it. You've had it before."

Selena slid the bottle up her thigh, and began rubbing the top of it against her vagina. She pushed it into her slit. Novalee looked away. Suddenly, Selena thrust the bottle into her face and waved it in front of her. "Want somethin' to kill the taste," she cackled. Selena was drunk, and she smelled. Novalee just wanted to get away from her. She decided to go and wake Marty. She stood up and turned towards the hall. Selena followed her.

"You fuckin', twat!" she screamed. "Ain't I good enough for ya no more?" Selena swung the bottle at the back of Novalee's head. The blow caused the bottle to shatter, and it split Novalee's head wide open. Her knees buckled, and she went down.

When Novalee opened her eyes, a crushing pain shot through her head. She was in the living room, her hands and feet, tied behind her back. "So, you're still alive, are ya," she heard Selena drawl. Novalee could see that Selena had blood on her hands, and she was holding a knife.

Selena helped her to kneel upright, and she sat on the backs of her legs. She felt woozy, but she tried to scream for Marty. "Scream all you want, lover," Selena taunted. "Marty won't be wakin' up anytime soon." Selena knew he would.

Novalee tried to reason with her, almost knowing what the answer would be. "Just let me leave here, and you can have Marty," she cried.

Selena laughed. "I've always had Marty, you little slut...and now, I'm gonna have my way with you!"

Novalee was sweating, and she began to shiver. She was beginning to feel sick, and she started to fall over. Selena grabbed her by the hair and pulled her up. She crouched down in front of her and pouted, "Let me get that hot shirt off of you." She began to slice up the front of Novalee's tank top, and her breasts fell out, exposed for Selena to see. She ripped Novalee's shirt the rest of the way off and poked her nipples with the tip of the knife. "Mmmm...very nice," she mused. She licked Novalee's cheek and pressed the knife against her throat. She began to trace a circle around the pink flesh of her areola. Suddenly, she pushed the knife's point into her nipple, and blood appeared instantly.

Novalee screamed in pain, and Selena seemed to be getting aroused by her own actions. She lowered the knife and sliced across Novalee's belly. She began to cry, and she begged Selena to let her go. "Please, stop this, Selena! Oh, God it hurts!"

Selena began to suck the blood from her nipple. When she tried to kiss her, Novalee pulled away. Selena punched her, hard, in the face. Her nose began to bleed, and she started to pass out. Selena had become uncontrollably aroused. Still holding the knife, she slid her hands down her belly, and began clutching at her crotch. Suddenly, she heard Marty calling from his room, and she stood up. She told Novalee, "I'll be back, sweetie...don't you worry." And she went down the hall.

10

Marty had awoken from his drug induced coma. Still in a stupor, he was unsure of where he was. Slowly, he began to realize that he was tied to the bed. "One of Selena's games," he thought. He remembered that he had been watching one of his movies. He could see that the projector was still on.

Novalee was almost unconscious, but she had heard Marty, too. She tried to get her head to stop spinning, and regain her composure. "Marty, help me!" she cried. She tried to push herself across the floor, and she screamed again. "Marty, please...she's killing me!"

"Where are you?" he yelled. He knew Selena was out of her mind, but he still couldn't imagine the horror that she was about to inflict. He struggled to get out of his own restraints, but it was useless.

Amused at the situation, Selena walked into his room and climbed up on top of him. Marty was livid. "Where is she?" he demanded. "What have you done?"

"Ohh...nothing," she lied mischievously. "But I'm gonna take care of her, and then I'll be back to see you."

She started to leave, and he said, "I've had enough of this shit...cut me loose!"

At that, her mood changed. "You make me sick!" she snarled, and slapped him in the mouth.

Marty tried to clear his head. "What are you gonna do?"

She thought for a second, and then she said, "I'm gonna make us feel real good." She began to press herself into his crotch, and she lifted her shirt over her head. She threw it on the floor and leaned forward to push her tongue into his mouth. She bit his lip and ran her tongue down to his chest, biting his nipple. She sat up, and continued to undulate over him, pulling her hair back behind her head. She closed her eyes, and for a moment, she looked like the girl he'd known, so many months before. But he quickly snapped back to reality and growled, "What the fuck! What is going on here? Untie me...you fucking, whore!"

Selena was getting agitated. "Ohh, now see what you're doing! You're ruining all the fun! Are you still worried about that little witch? It's nothing. We had a fight, and she got over it. She'll be fine. Now, where were we?"

Marty wasn't sure where they were. As stoned as he'd been, it could have all been a dream. He'd had enough, though. "When I get loose from here, it's gonna be my turn..."

Selena was about to snap. Marty was beginning to bug her, and her head began to spin. "All he thinks about is that little whore," she thought. She closed her eyes and took a deep breath. "Stay in control," she told herself. But Selena was far from in control.

She began to prepare a fix, and again, Marty ordered her to let him go. She just ignored him and continued what she was doing. "I'll get you for this!" he threatened.

She turned to him and said, "No... you won't ...but God will." She tried to stick his arm, but he began to struggle. "You're going to make me miss," she said, gritting her teeth.

"Fuck you, bitch!" Marty groaned.

Selena had become completely angered, by now. She sat on his chest and slammed the needle into his arm. Marty's eyes rolled back into his head, and instantly, he relaxed. She pulled the syringe from his arm and snickered, "He doesn't know what's good for him." She went over to the movie projector and started the film. "Enjoy it, Marty. It might be your last."

11

Novalee knew that she would have to do something to save herself. She was in bad shape, but she was still alive. She thought about Marty, and his stupid movies. She decided that she would have to act, and it would have to be the role of a lifetime. Selena had come back down the hall, and was about to lay into her again.

"Please, Selena...don't!" she begged. "I'm really sorry for being bad. I...I love you."

Selena hesitated and said, "What the hell? Why, you little..."

Novalee continued, "I'm real horny, Selena... and I want you. Please, baby...let's make love." Selena started to think about it and Novalee went on. "I do love you, Selena. Please, believe me."

Selena was becoming very aroused. She stood over Novalee and cut her free. She helped her to her feet, and into the bathroom. Novalee could barely walk, and was shivering terribly. She sat on the toilet and vomited on herself. Selena went to Marty's room to cook up a fix.

Novalee almost fell off the toilet, as the juice ran through her veins. But within a few minutes, she began to feel better. Selena drew her a bath, and she climbed in. Almost grateful, Novalee thanked her and smiled. "Won't you join me?"

As they stood in the tub, they began to pay special attention to certain areas of their bodies. Novalee tenderly washed Selena's breasts, as Selena did the same to her vagina and bum. Soon Novalee began to lick and bite Selena's nipples. They began to kiss, tenderly at first, and then they became wild, as their arousal began to heighten. Selena pushed her fingers into Novalee's vagina. She moaned and her legs went weak. They finished their bath and moved to the bedroom.

Afterward, as Novalee brushed Selena's hair, she asked her if she wanted a drink. She said that she did, and Novalee said, "Two screwdrivers... coming right up."

Novalee's plan had been working up to that point. But she got greedy, and made a fatal mistake. She should have waited until Selena fell asleep, before she tried to leave. Selena began to notice that she had been gone for awhile, and decided to see what she was up too. When she came down the hall, she saw that Novalee had dressed, and was about to go out the back door. In a split second, Selena had grabbed her knife, and was in the kitchen. "You lyin', whore!" she screamed, and began to plunge the knife into Novalee's back. She tried to turn and grab Selena's arm, but the knife sliced across her hand, cutting off one of her fingers.

Novalee screamed, "Somebody, help me!" But no one could hear her. She managed to shove Selena, and started towards Marty's room, but Selena caught her in the living room and pulled her by the hair. She spun around, and Selena slammed the knife into her belly, and then into her crotch. Novalee dropped to her knees and held her stomach. She began to make gurgling sounds, and blood trickled from her mouth. She looked up at Selena, and tried to speak.

Selena teased her, "What...bitch? Tryin' to tell me somethin'. Why don't you drop dead." In another minute, Novalee was gone.

Satisfied with what she'd done, Selena lit up a cigarette. She took a few long puffs and blew the smoke out slowly. She stood there looking at Novalee, as if she were appreciating a piece of artwork. She took another drag from her cigarette and flicked it at Novalee's lifeless body. It bounced off of her, and extinguished in a pool of blood.

She snickered and turned to leave. Their love making, flashing through her mind. "Bitch," she muttered, and walked down the hall to Marty's room. "Now, I have him back," she thought to herself. "I don't know, what he ever saw in her."

12

To keep Marty out of it all day, Selena had to give him some really heavy doses. There was enough in the stash for one more, really strong fix. She decided to do it all, and really screw herself up. She pushed the needle into her arm and watched, as the syringe emptied into her vein. Within an instant, she began to stagger back into the dresser. She started to go down, and struggled to reach the bed.

Selena crawled up on top of Marty, and laid motionless for a moment. She fought to get a grip on herself and not pass out. As her composure began to return, she could hear his heart beating. It sounded very strange to her. Like it was a million miles away.

Marty's film had still been running, and had come to the end of the reel. It made a flapping noise, and startled her, though stoned as she was. She pushed herself up and sat on Marty's crotch. She began to grind herself against him. "C'mon, lover...give it to me. Fuck me!

Make...me...cum!" But he wasn't responding, and he was barely breathing. Selena patted him on the chest and cried, "Not yet, Marty!" She had wanted them to die together—in an orgasmic curtain call. She picked up the scissors that had been lying on the bed and pressed the point into her belly. Blood began to run out of her, and down between her legs. For a moment she felt scared.

She pulled the scissors out of her belly and cut a deep slice into her wrist. Blood spurted everywhere. Marty began to mumble, and he seemed to be gasping for breath. Selena became enraged at him, and started stabbing him in the chest. Then, she began plunging the scissors into herself. She screamed at Marty to fuck her. Feverishly, she grinded herself against him. "Make me cum...you bastard!" Selena felt a warm feeling beginning to come over her. The room seemed to be getting darker. Her vision was blurred, and it was getting harder to breathe.

She felt weak, and couldn't hold herself up anymore. She fell onto Marty's chest, and as she became more confused, she began to lick the blood from him. She sucked at his wounds, and blood dripped from her lips. She licked and licked, and tried to clean Marty up, but the blood kept draining out of both of them. "There's just too much for me," she thought. Selena tried to get up, but she couldn't move. She gazed out the window and thought, "How strange... there are no stars."

13

It had been several hours, since the sun had gone down, on a dreamy October evening in El Paso, Texas. A happy couple sat on their front steps and looked up at the stars. Liz looked at the wedding band on her finger. She had finally gotten what she'd wanted all along. She had loved Marty since they were kids. She picked the brightest star that she could find and made a wish. She hoped that things would be different this time and vowed to keep the man she cherished, even though she knew, that she'd have to give much more, than she'd receive.

Marty had somehow known that he'd wind up with Liz. "We were meant to be together," he thought. He realized that he was lucky to be sitting where he was. Very lucky, indeed.

Bruce had come by the house the morning after Selena's bloody rampage, with the intention of giving his friend another chance with the band. He had looked in the window and saw Novalee's body on the living room floor. He called the police, and an ambulance arrived in time for medics to stabilize Marty. It turned out that his wounds hadn't been serious enough to kill him. Between his statement, and the detective's investigation, he was cleared of any wrong doing, in the deaths of the two women.

A sweep of the house did however, uncover small amounts of what one cop described as, "Every drug known to mankind." Marty avoided jail time by agreeing to seek help. After a few days in the hospital, and a month long stay in a court appointed drug rehabilitation facility, he was free to start living again.

And he did get to play on that first album, as well as a six week tour of dates the band played, at the end of summer. But that was enough for Marty. He didn't want to live that kind of life, anymore. He left the band—on his own this time. Somehow, Bruce understood.

At twenty five, he'd seen and done more than most people his age. Now, he knew that it was time to settle down. His only regret was that he'd never dare to have a child with Liz, and there would be no one to carry on his legacy.

At the very same moment, miles across the Atlantic Ocean, a four year old boy played in his back yard. A woman named Claudia, came to the kitchen door and called her son, to come in for lunch. She smiled lovingly, as he ran towards her. He playfully smacked her on the butt, as he went past her into the house. "Why, you little brat," she laughed. "You're going to be just like your father."

www.ingramcontent.com/pod-product-compliance
Lightning Source LLC
Chambersburg PA
CBHW030317180626
46810CB00003B/1114